Measure for Measure

DOVER · THRIFT · EDITIONS

Measure for Measure

WILLIAM SHAKESPEARE

DOVER PUBLICATIONS, INC.
Mineola, New York

DOVER THRIFT EDITIONS

GENERAL EDITOR: PAUL NEGRI
EDITOR OF THIS VOLUME: KATHY CASEY

Copyright

Copyright © 1999 by Dover Publications, Inc.
All rights reserved under Pan American and International Copyright Conventions.

Published in Canada by General Publishing Company, Ltd., 30 Lesmill Road, Don Mills, Toronto, Ontario.

Theatrical Rights

This Dover Thrift Edition may be used in its entirety, in adaptation, or in any other way for theatrical productions, professional and amateur, in the United States, without permission, fee, or acknowledgment. (This may not apply outside of the United States, as copyright conditions may vary.)

Bibliographical Note

This Dover edition, first published in 1999, contains the unabridged text of *Measure for Measure* as published in Volume VI of *The Caxton Edition of the Complete Works of William Shakespeare*, Caxton Publishing Company, London, n.d. The Note was prepared for this edition, and explanatory footnotes from the Caxton edition have been revised.

Library of Congress Cataloging-in-Publication Data

Shakespeare, William, 1564–1616.
    Measure for measure / William Shakespeare.
        p.   cm. — (Dover thrift editions)
    ISBN 0-486-40889-2 (pbk.)
    1. Chastity—Law and legislation—Austria—Vienna—Drama.   2. Brothers and sisters—Austria—Vienna—Drama.   I. Title.   II. Series.
PR2824.A1   1999
822.3'3—dc21   99-29893
                                                                                                              CIP

Manufactured in the United States of America
Dover Publications, Inc., 31 East 2nd Street, Mineola, N.Y. 11501

Note

Measure for Measure, one of three of Shakespeare's plays classed as "dark comedies" or tragicomedies, resonates with contemporary issues such as religious beliefs embodied in laws, and public standards of morality in contrast with actual behavior at all levels of society. More than any of his other plays, it examines the interplay of society and government. At the same time, it probes the psychology of a pivotal character, Angelo.

The play probably was first staged in 1604, early in the reign of King James I. Two speeches in it appear to allude to this king's notorious dislike of having crowds of his well-wishing subjects surround him in public.

Measure for Measure is set in 16th-century Vienna, where longtime lax enforcement of strict laws has led to sexual licentiousness and general corruption. Duke Vincentio, pretending that he must leave the city on urgent business, appoints Angelo, a lord with a reputation for great rectitude, to enforce the laws in his absence. Then, disguised as a friar, he secretly intervenes with those principally affected by Angelo's harsh, selective application of the law, as Angelo abuses his power without restraint. Being authorized to condemn or to grant mercy, Angelo proves to be no more able to resist temptation than was young Claudio, whom he has condemned to die for a transgression that is slight in comparison with his own.

The play explores difficult and disturbing questions of personal morality, the responsibilities of those who govern, the nature of justice and guilt, sexual mores and religious prescription, and the need for mercy in judging others. Two of the central characters, Angelo and Isabella, who firmly believe in moral absolutes, are forced to confront ambiguity, uncertainty, and, in Angelo's case, his own hypocrisy. The assumption that the government should enforce established religious strictures on sexual behavior underlies all aspects of the action.

The plot of *Measure for Measure* relies on three common folktale elements: the corrupt judge; the ruler who, disguised, observes others' actions unknown to them; and the secret substitution of one person for another in a clandestine sexual tryst. Specifically, the main source of the play's plot was *Promos and Cassandra*, written by George Whetstone before 1578, which in turn was based upon an Italian story by Giraldo Cinthio in his 1565 *Hecatommithi*.

Contents

Dramatis Personæ   x

Act I   1

Act II   15

Act III   36

Act IV   52

Act V   68

Dramatis Personæ[1]

VINCENTIO, the Duke.

ANGELO, Deputy.

ESCALUS, an ancient Lord.

CLAUDIO, a young gentleman.

LUCIO, a fantastic.

Two other gentlemen.

PROVOST.

THOMAS, } two friars.
PETER,

A Justice.

VARRIUS.

ELBOW, a simple constable.

FROTH, a foolish gentleman.

POMPEY, servant to Mistress Overdone.

ABHORSON, an executioner.

BARNARDINE, a dissolute prisoner.

ISABELLA, sister to Claudio.

MARIANA, betrothed to Angelo.

JULIET, beloved of Claudio.

FRANCISCA, a nun.

MISTRESS OVERDONE, a bawd.

Lords, Officers, Citizens, Boy, and Attendants.

SCENE—*Vienna*

---

[1]This play was first printed in the First Folio. It was there divided into acts and scenes. At the end of the text, the scene was described as Vienna, and the names of all the actors were given.

ACT I.

SCENE I. *An Apartment in the Duke's Palace.*

Enter DUKE, ESCALUS, Lords, *and* Attendants

DUKE.   Escalus.
ESCAL.   My lord.
DUKE.   Of government the properties to unfold,
       Would seem in me to affect speech[1] and discourse;
       Since I am put to know[2] that your own science
       Exceeds, in that, the lists of all advice
       My strength can give you: then no more remains,
       But that to your sufficiency . . . . .
       . . . . as your worth is able,
       And let them work.[3] The nature of our people,
       Our city's institutions, and the terms
       For common justice,[4] you're as pregnant in
       As art and practice[5] hath enriched any
       That we remember. There is our commission,
       From which we would not have you warp. Call hither,
       I say, bid come before us Angelo.   [*Exit an* Attendant.
       What figure of us[6] think you he will bear?
       For you must know, we have with special soul[7]
       Elected him our absence to supply;

---

[1] *to affect speech*] to love talk for its own sake.
[2] *I am put to know*] Cf. 2 *Hen. VI*, III, i, 43: "Had I been first *put* [*i.e.*, compelled] to speak."
[3] *then no more remains . . . work*] This is obscure, and it is usually assumed that some words accidentally have been dropped out. Theobald inserted in the dotted spaces *you add Due diligency*, for which Spedding substituted *I add Commission ample.*
[4] *the terms . . . justice*] the technical language of the courts.
[5] *art and practice*] Cf. *Hen. V*, I, i, 51: "*art and practic* part of life."
[6] *figure of us*] resemblance to us.
[7] *with special soul*] out of my special affection for him.

1

    Lent him our terror, dress'd him with our love,
    And given his deputation all the organs
    Of our own power: what think you of it?
ESCAL.   If any in Vienna be of worth
    To undergo such ample grace and honour,
    It is Lord Angelo.
DUKE.   Look where he comes.

Enter ANGELO

ANG.   Always obedient to your Grace's will,
    I come to know your pleasure.
DUKE.   Angelo,
    There is a kind of character in thy life,
    That to th' observer doth thy history
    Fully unfold. Thyself and thy belongings
    Are not thine own so proper,[8] as to waste
    Thyself upon thy virtues, they on thee.
    Heaven doth with us as we with torches do,
    Not light them for themselves; for if our virtues
    Did not go forth of us, 't were all alike
    As if we had them not. Spirits are not finely touch'd
    But to fine issues;[9] nor Nature never lends
    The smallest scruple of her excellence,
    But, like a thrifty goddess, she determines
    Herself the glory of a creditor,
    Both thanks and use.[10] But I do bend my speech
    To one that can my part in him advertise;[11]
    Hold therefore, Angelo:—
    In our remove[12] be thou at full ourself;
    Mortality and mercy[13] in Vienna
    Live in thy tongue and heart: old Escalus,
    Though first in question, is thy secondary.[14]
    Take thy commission.

[8]*thine own so proper*] so exclusively thine own property.
[9]*Spirits . . . issues*] The soul is not endowed with nobleness, but for realizing noble purposes.
[10]*she determines . . . use*] she allots to herself the creditor's splendid advantages both of gratitude for service rendered and of interest on the loan.
[11]*can . . . advertise*] can give instruction as to the part of deputy which I bestow on him. *Advertise* is accented on the second syllable.
[12]*In our remove*] On our withdrawal.
[13]*Mortality and mercy*] Power of capital punishment and of granting pardon.
[14]*Though . . . secondary*] Though he was first under consideration for this post, [Escalus] now is thy subordinate.

ANG.   Now, good my lord,
    Let there be some more test made of my metal,
    Before so noble and so great a figure
    Be stamp'd upon it.
DUKE.   No more evasion:
    We have with a leaven'd[15] and prepared choice
    Proceeded to you; therefore take your honours.
    Our haste from hence is of so quick condition,
    That it prefers itself, and leaves unquestion'd[16]
    Matters of needful value. We shall write to you,
    As time and our concernings shall importune,
    How it goes with us; and do look to know
    What doth befall you here. So, fare you well:
    To the hopeful execution do I leave you
    Of your commissions.
ANG.   Yet, give leave, my lord,
    That we may bring you something on the way.
DUKE.   My haste may not admit it;
    Nor need you, on mine honour, have to do
    With any scruple; your scope is as mine own,
    So to enforce or qualify the laws
    As to your soul seems good. Give me your hand:
    I'll privily away. I love the people,[17]
    But do not like to stage me to their eyes:
    Though it do well, I do not relish well
    Their loud applause and Aves vehement;
    Nor do I think the man of safe discretion
    That does affect it. Once more, fare you well.
ANG.   The heavens give safety to your purposes!
ESCAL.   Lead forth and bring you back in happiness!
DUKE.   I thank you. Fare you well.   [*Exit.*
ESCAL.   I shall desire you, sir, to give me leave
    To have free speech with you; and it concerns me
    To look into the bottom of my place:
    A power I have, but of what strength and nature
    I am not yet instructed.
ANG.   'T is so with me. Let us withdraw together,

---

[15]*leaven'd*] well fermented, mature.
[16]*prefers . . . unquestion'd*] takes precedence of everything else, and leaves undiscussed.
[17]*I love the people, etc.*] Shakespeare is commonly credited here with an allusion to King James I's notorious dislike of demonstrations in his honor by crowds in public places.

And we may soon our satisfaction have
Touching that point.

ESCAL. I'll wait upon your honour. [*Exeunt.*

SCENE II. *A Street.*

Enter LUCIO *and two* Gentlemen

LUCIO. If the Duke, with the other dukes, come not to composition with the King of Hungary, why then all the dukes fall upon the king.

FIRST GENT. Heaven grant us its peace, but not the King of Hungary's!

SEC. GENT. Amen.

LUCIO. Thou concludest like the sanctimonious pirate, that went to sea with the Ten Commandments, but scraped one out of the table.

SEC. GENT. "Thou shalt not steal"?

LUCIO. Ay, that he razed.

FIRST GENT. Why, 't was a commandment to command the captain and all the rest from their functions: they put forth to steal. There's not a soldier of us all, that, in the thanksgiving before meat, do relish the petition well that prays for peace.

SEC. GENT. I never heard any soldier dislike[1] it.

LUCIO. I believe thee; for I think thou never wast where grace was said.

SEC. GENT. No? a dozen times at least.

FIRST GENT. What, in metre?

LUCIO. In any proportion[2] or in any language.

FIRST GENT. I think, or in any religion.

LUCIO. Ay, why not? Grace is grace, despite of all controversy: as, for example, thou thyself art a wicked villain, despite of all grace.

FIRST GENT. Well, there went but a pair of shears between us.[3]

LUCIO. I grant; as there may between the lists and the velvet. Thou art the list.

FIRST GENT. And thou the velvet: thou art good velvet; thou'rt a

---

[1] *dislike*] express dislike. Cf. *As You Like It*, V, iv, 66.

[2] *proportion*] measure.

[3] *Well, there went . . . us*] we are of the same piece; a proverbial expression suggesting that men are all alike save for the tailor's interposition. Cf. Marston's *Malcontent*, 1604, IV, 2 (ed. Bullen, I, 290): "*There goes but a pair of shears* betwixt an emperor and the son of a bagpiper."

three-piled[4] piece, I warrant thee: I had as lief be a list of an English kersey, as be piled, as thou art piled, for a French velvet.[5] Do I speak feelingly now?

LUCIO.   I think thou dost; and, indeed, with most painful feeling of thy speech: I will, out of thine own confession, learn to begin thy health;[6] but, whilst I live, forget to drink after thee.

FIRST GENT.   I think I have done myself wrong, have I not?

SEC. GENT.   Yes, that thou hast, whether thou art tainted or free.

LUCIO.   Behold, behold, where Madam Mitigation comes! I have purchased as many diseases under her roof as come to—

SEC. GENT.   To what, I pray?

LUCIO.   Judge.

SEC. GENT.   To three thousand dolours a year.

FIRST GENT.   Ay, and more.

LUCIO.   A French crown[7] more.

FIRST GENT.   Thou art always figuring diseases in me; but thou art full of error; I am sound.

LUCIO.   Nay, not as one would say, healthy; but so sound as things that are hollow: thy bones are hollow; impiety has made a feast of thee.

Enter MISTRESS OVERDONE

FIRST GENT.   How now! which of your hips has the most profound sciatica?

MRS. OV.   Well, well; there's one yonder arrested and carried to prison was worth five thousand of you all.

SEC. GENT.   Who's that, I pray thee?

MRS. OV.   Marry, sir, that's Claudio, Signior Claudio.

FIRST GENT.   Claudio to prison? 't is not so.

MRS. OV.   Nay, but I know 't is so: I saw him arrested; saw him carried away; and, which is more, within these three days his head to be chopped off.

LUCIO.   But, after all this fooling, I would not have it so. Art thou sure of this?

MRS. OV.   I am too sure of it: and it is for getting Madam Julietta with child.

LUCIO.   Believe me, this may be: he promised to meet me two hours since, and he was ever precise in promise-keeping.

---

[4]*three-piled*] Cf. *All's Well*, IV, v, 88.

[5]*piled . . . velvet*] a pun on "piled" in the sense of "peeled," made bald (by the French venereal disease), and "piled," richly woven (of velvet).

[6]*begin thy health*] begin drinking to the recovery of thy health.

[7]*A French crown*] A bald pate. Cf. *Mids. N. Dr.*, I, ii, 86: "Some of your *French crowns have no hair* at all." There is a tacit allusion to the medical term, "corona veneris."

SEC. GENT.   Besides, you know, it draws something near to the speech we had to such a purpose.

FIRST GENT.   But, most of all, agreeing with the proclamation.

LUCIO.   Away! let's go learn the truth of it.

                                    [*Exeunt* LUCIO *and* Gentlemen.

MRS. OV.   Thus, what with the war, what with the sweat,[8] what with the gallows, and what with poverty, I am custom-shrunk.

Enter POMPEY

     How now! what's the news with you?

POM.   Yonder man is carried to prison.

MRS. OV.   Well; what has he done?

POM.   A woman.

MRS. OV.   But what's his offence?

POM.   Groping for trouts in a peculiar[9] river.

MRS. OV.   What, is there a maid with child by him?

POM.   No, but there's a woman with maid by him. You have not heard of the proclamation, have you?

MRS. OV.   What proclamation, man?

POM.   All houses in the suburbs of Vienna must be plucked down.

MRS. OV.   And what shall become of those in the city?

POM.   They shall stand for seed: they had gone down too, but that a wise burgher put in for them.

MRS. OV.   But shall all our houses of resort in the suburbs[10] be pulled down?

POM.   To the ground, mistress.

MRS. OV.   Why, here's a change indeed in the commonwealth! What shall become of me?

POM.   Come; fear not you: good counsellors lack no clients: though you change your place, you need not change your trade; I'll be your tapster still. Courage! there will be pity taken on you: you that have worn your eyes almost out in the service, you will be considered.

MRS. OV.   What's to do here, Thomas tapster?[11] let's withdraw.

POM.   Here comes Signior Claudio, led by the provost to prison; and there's Madam Juliet.

                                            [*Exeunt.*

---

[8]*sweat*] probably the recent epidemic of the "sweating sickness." A reference to the "sweating tub" methods of curing venereal disease would be less pertinent.

[9]*peculiar*] in private ownership.

[10]*All houses in the suburbs*] Disorderly houses in Elizabethan London were usually located in the districts outside the city boundaries.

[11]*Thomas tapster*] A colloquial class-name, like Tom Tinker or Tom Tosspot, playfully applied here to Pompey.

Enter PROVOST, CLAUDIO, JULIET, *and* Officers

CLAUD.   Fellow, why dost thou show me thus to the world?
    Bear me to prison, where I am committed.
PROV.   I do it not in evil disposition,
    But from Lord Angelo by special charge.
CLAUD.   Thus can the demigod Authority
    Make us pay down for our offence by weight
    The words of heaven;—on whom it will, it will;
    On whom it will not, so;[12] yet still 't is just.

Re-enter LUCIO *and two* Gentlemen

LUCIO.   Why, how now, Claudio! whence comes this restraint?
CLAUD.   From too much liberty, my Lucio, liberty:
    As surfeit is the father of much fast,
    So every scope by the immoderate use
    Turns to restraint. Our natures do pursue,
    Like rats that ravin down their proper bane,
    A thirsty evil; and when we drink we die.[13]
LUCIO.   If I could speak so wisely under an arrest, I would send for
    certain of my creditors: and yet, to say the truth, I had as lief have
    the foppery of freedom as the morality[14] of imprisonment. What's
    thy offence, Claudio?
CLAUD.   What but to speak of would offend again.
LUCIO.   What, is 't murder?
CLAUD.   No.
LUCIO.   Lechery?
CLAUD.   Call it so.
PROV.   Away, sir! you must go.
CLAUD.   One word, good friend. Lucio, a word with you.
LUCIO.   A hundred, if they'll do you any good.
    Is lechery so look'd after?

---

[12]*The words of heaven . . . it will not, so*] This, the punctuation of the Folios, is clearly
right. Authority can make us suffer for our offence precisely the retribution described
in the Bible. The Scriptural words to which "on whom it will," etc., allude, are in two
verses in Romans ix: (v. 15) "For He saith to Moses: 'I will have mercy *on whom I will*
have mercy,'" and (v. 18) "Therefore hath He mercy *on whom He will* have mercy."
[13]*Our natures . . . we die*] Cf. Chapman's adaptation of the same image in his *Revenge
for Honour*, II, i, 113–115: ". . . men like poison'd rats, which when they've swallowed
The pleasing bane, rest not until they drink, And can rest then much less until they
burst with 't."
[14]*morality*] Sir William D'Avenant's happy change (in his *Law for Lovers*, an adapted
version of the play) for the Folio reading *mortality*.

CLAUD.   Thus stands it with me: upon a true contract[15]
    I got possession of Julietta's bed:
    You know the lady; she is fast my wife,
    Save that we do the denunciation lack
    Of outward order: this we came not to,
    Only for propagation of a dower[16]
    Remaining in the coffer of her friends;
    From whom we thought it meet to hide our love
    Till time had made them for us.[17] But it chances
    The stealth of our most mutual entertainment
    With character too gross is writ on Juliet.
LUCIO.   With child, perhaps?
CLAUD.   Unhappily, even so.
    And the new Deputy now for the Duke,—
    Whether it be the fault and glimpse of newness,[18]
    Or whether that the body public be
    A horse whereon the governor doth ride,
    Who, newly in the seat, that it may know
    He can command, lets it straight feel the spur;
    Whether the tyranny be in his place,
    Or in his eminence that fills it up,
    I stagger in:—but this new governor
    Awakes me all the enrolled penalties
    Which have, like unscour'd armour, hung by the wall
    So long, that nineteen zodiacs[19] have gone round,
    And none of them been worn; and, for a name,
    Now puts the drowsy and neglected act
    Freshly on me: 't is surely for a name.
LUCIO.   I warrant it is: and thy head stands so tickle on thy shoulders,
    that a milkmaid, if she be in love, may sigh it off. Send after the
    Duke, and appeal to him.
CLAUD.   I have done so, but he's not to be found.
    I prithee, Lucio, do me this kind service:

[15]*true contract*] a genuine contract (accented on the second syllable) of betrothal, which preceded the marriage rites. The ceremony of the contract is fully described in *Tw. Night*, V, i, 150–155.

[16]*we do the denunciation . . . dower*] we are without the formal ceremony of public announcement (of our union); this we deferred merely to allow of some increase in the amount of the lady's dowry.

[17]*Till time . . . for us*] Until time had reconciled her friends to our purpose.

[18]*fault . . . newness*] inherent defect and hasty vision of one in a new position.

[19]*nineteen zodiacs*] In the next scene the Duke declares he has suffered the law to be in abeyance not *nineteen*, but *fourteen* years. The dramatist may have meant that the Duke had reigned only fourteen of those nineteen years.

This day my sister should the cloister enter
And there receive her approbation:[20]
Acquaint her with the danger of my state;
Implore her, in my voice, that she make friends
To the strict deputy; bid herself assay him:
I have great hope in that; for in her youth
There is a prone[21] and speechless dialect,
Such as move men; beside, she hath prosperous art
When she will play with reason and discourse,
And well she can persuade.

LUCIO.   I pray she may; as well for the encouragement of the like,
which else would stand under grievous imposition,[22] as for the en-
joying of thy life, who I would be sorry should be thus foolishly
lost at a game of tick-tack.[23] I'll to her.

CLAUD.   I thank you, good friend Lucio.

LUCIO.   Within two hours.

CLAUD.   Come, officer, away!   [*Exeunt.*

SCENE III. *A Monastery.*

Enter DUKE *and* FRIAR THOMAS

DUKE.   No, holy father; throw away that thought;
Believe not that the dribbling dart of love
Can pierce a complete bosom.[1] Why I desire thee
To give me secret harbour, hath a purpose
More grave and wrinkled than the aims and ends
Of burning youth.

FRI. T.   May your grace speak of it?

DUKE.   My holy sir, none better knows than you
How I have ever loved the life removed,
And held in idle price to haunt assemblies
Where youth, and cost, and witless bravery keeps.

---

[20]*receive her approbation*] enter on her term of probation, her novitiate.

[21]*prone, etc.*] "Prone" seems here used in the sense of "prompt," or "apt." The sentence
means that youth has an aptitude to move or persuade without use of words. Cf. for
the thought, *Win. Tale*, II, ii, 41: "The *silence* often of pure innocence *Persuades*
when speaking fails."

[22]*stand under grievous imposition*] be liable to grievous penalties.

[23]*tick-tack*] A loose reference to a game resembling backgammon.

---

[1]*dribbling dart . . . complete bosom*] Love's weakly aimed, feebly fluttering arrow cannot
pierce a completely armed, self-possessed heart. In archery a "dribbler" is one who
does not aim well.

I have deliver'd to Lord Angelo,
A man of stricture and firm abstinence,
My absolute power and place here in Vienna,
And he supposes me travell'd to Poland;
For so I have strew'd it in the common ear,
And so it is received. Now, pious sir,
You will demand of me why I do this.

FRI. T.   Gladly, my lord.

DUKE.   We have strict statutes and most biting laws,
The needful bits and curbs to headstrong weeds,[2]
Which for this fourteen years we have let slip;[3]
Even like an o'ergrown lion in a cave,
That goes not out to prey. Now, as fond fathers,
Having bound up the threatening twigs of birch,
Only to stick it in their children's sight
For terror, not to use, in time the rod
Becomes[4] more mock'd than fear'd; so our decrees,
Dead to infliction, to themselves are dead;
And liberty plucks justice by the nose;
The baby beats the nurse, and quite athwart
Goes all decorum.

FRI. T.   It rested in your Grace
To unloose this tied-up justice when you pleased:
And it in you more dreadful would have seem'd
Than in Lord Angelo.

DUKE.   I do fear, too dreadful:
Sith 't was my fault to give the people scope,
'T would be my tyranny to strike and gall them
For what I bid them do: for we bid this be done,
When evil deeds have their permissive pass,
And not the punishment. Therefore, indeed, my father,
I have on Angelo imposed the office;
Who may, in the ambush of my name, strike home,
And yet my nature never in the fight

---

[2]*weeds*] This is the reading of the Folios, for which Theobald substituted *steeds*. The figure of rank and noisome growths that deface a neglected garden suits the context.

[3]*let slip*] D'Avenant (in his altered version, followed by Theobald and others) substituted *let sleep*, but "let slip" in the sense of "neglect," "suffer to pass unnoticed," is often found. Cf. *Tw. Night*, III, iv, 272: "Let the matter *slip*."

[4]*Becomes*] D'Avenant's version inserted this needed word, which is missing from the Folios.

To do in slander.[5] And to behold his sway,
I will, as 't were a brother of your order,
Visit both prince and people: therefore, I prithee,
Supply me with the habit, and instruct me
How I may formally in person bear me
Like a true friar. More reasons for this action
At our more leisure shall I render you;
Only, this one: Lord Angelo is precise;
Stands at a guard with envy;[6] scarce confesses
That his blood flows, or that his appetite
Is more to bread than stone: hence shall we see,
If power change purpose, what our seemers be.[7]   [Exeunt.

Scene IV. A Nunnery.

Enter Isabella *and* Francisca

Isab.   And have you nuns no farther privileges?
Fran.   Are not these large enough?
Isab.   Yes, truly: I speak not as desiring more;
  But rather wishing a more strict restraint
  Upon the sisterhood, the votarists of Saint Clare.
Lucio.   [within]. Ho! Peace be in this place!
Isab.   Who's that which calls?
Fran.   It is a man's voice. Gentle Isabella,
  Turn you the key, and know his business of him;
  You may, I may not; you are yet unsworn.
  When you have vow'd, you must not speak with men
  But in the presence of the prioress:
  Then, if you speak, you must not show your face;
  Or, if you show your face, you must not speak.
  He calls again; I pray you, answer him.   [Exit.
Isab.   Peace and prosperity! Who is 't that calls?

Enter Lucio

---

[5]*And yet . . . slander*] This is the original reading. Pope substituted *sight* for *fight*, Theobald *so do* for *to do*, and Hammer *it slander* for *in slander*. The meaning seems to be that the Duke's person will not figure in Angelo's war with crime, so as to incur injurious comments (either for past mildness or present sternness).
[6]*Stands at a guard with envy*] Stands on his guard against, is able to defend himself against, malicious tongues.
[7]*hence . . . be*] The Duke will discover whether the possession of power works any change in Angelo's character, whether men are really what they seem to be.

LUCIO.   Hail, virgin, if you be, as those cheek-roses
     Proclaim you are no less! Can you so stead me
     As bring me to the sight of Isabella,
     A novice of this place, and the fair sister
     To her unhappy brother Claudio?
ISAB.   Why, "her unhappy brother"? let me ask
     The rather, for I now must make you know
     I am that Isabella and his sister.
LUCIO.   Gentle and fair, your brother kindly greets you:
     Not to be weary with you, he's in prison.
ISAB.   Woe me! for what?
LUCIO.   For that which, if myself might be his judge,
     He should receive his punishment in thanks:
     He hath got his friend with child.
ISAB.   Sir, make me not your story.[1]
LUCIO.   It is true.
     I would not—though 't is my familiar sin
     With maids to seem the lapwing,[2] and to jest,
     Tongue far from heart—play with all virgins so:
     I hold you as a thing ensky'd and sainted;
     By your renouncement, an immortal spirit;
     And to be talk'd with in sincerity,
     As with a saint.
ISAB.   You do blaspheme the good in mocking me.
LUCIO.   Do you believe it. Fewness and truth,[3] 't is thus:—
     Your brother and his lover have embraced:
     As those that feed grow full,—as blossoming time,
     That from the seedness the bare fallow brings
     To teeming foison,—even so her plenteous womb
     Expresseth his full tilth and husbandry.[4]
ISAB.   Some one with child by him?—My cousin Juliet?
LUCIO.   Is she your cousin?
ISAB.   Adoptedly; as school-maids change their names
     By vain, though apt, affection.
LUCIO.   She it is.
ISAB.   O, let him marry her.

---

[1]*make me not your story*] make me not your subject of mirth, your jest. Cf. *M. Wives*, V, v, 154: "I am your *theme*."

[2]*lapwing*] The "lapwing" or peewit often figures as the symbol of fickleness and inconstancy, because of its wily habits.

[3]*Fewness and truth*] Briefly and truly.

[4]*womb . . . husbandry*] Cf. *Sonnet* iii, 5–6: "whose unear'd *womb* disdains the *tillage* of thy *husbandry.*"

LUCIO.   This is the point.
    The duke is very strangely gone from hence;
    Bore many gentlemen, myself being one,
    In hand, and hope of action:[5] but we do learn
    By those that know the very nerves of state,
    His givings-out were of an infinite distance
    From his true-meant design. Upon his place,
    And with full line of his authority,
    Governs Lord Angelo; a man whose blood
    Is very snow-broth; one who never feels
    The wanton stings and motions of the sense,
    But doth rebate[6] and blunt his natural edge
    With profits of the mind, study and fast.
    He—to give fear to use and liberty,[7]
    Which have for long run by the hideous law,
    As mice by lions—hath pick'd out an act,
    Under whose heavy sense your brother's life
    Falls into forfeit: he arrests him on it;
    And follows close the rigour of the statute,
    To make him an example. All hope is gone,
    Unless you have the grace by your fair prayer
    To soften Angelo: and that's my pith of business
    'Twixt you and your poor brother.
ISAB.   Doth he so seek his life?
LUCIO.   Has censured him
    Already; and, as I hear, the provost hath
    A warrant for his execution.
ISAB.   Alas! what poor ability 's in me
    To do him good?
LUCIO.   Assay the power you have.
ISAB.   My power? Alas, I doubt,—
LUCIO.   Our doubts are traitors,
    And make us lose the good we oft might win
    By fearing to attempt. Go to Lord Angelo,
    And let him learn to know, when maidens sue,
    Men give like gods; but when they weep and kneel,
    All their petitions are as freely theirs
    As they themselves would owe[8] them.

[5]*Bore . . . action*] Deluded and raised false hopes of action. For "*and* hope of action" editors sometimes substitute "*with*" or "*in* hope of action," a construction harmonizing better with the common phrase "bear in hand," *i.e.*, "delude."

[6]*rebate*] "Rebate" and "blunt" mean the same thing.

[7]*to give fear . . . liberty*] to offer the restraint of fear to habit and license.

[8]*owe*] have. "Owe" is commonly used for "own," "possess."

ISAB.   I'll see what I can do.
LUCIO.   But speedily.
ISAB.   I will about it straight;
        No longer staying but to give the Mother
        Notice of my affair. I humbly thank you:
        Commend me to my brother: soon at night
        I'll send him certain word of my success.
LUCIO.   I take my leave of you.
ISAB.   Good sir, adieu.   [*Exeunt.*

ACT II.

SCENE I. *A Hall in Angelo's House.*

Enter ANGELO, ESCALUS, *and a* Justice, PROVOST, Officers, *and other* Attendants, *behind*

ANGELO.   We must not make a scarecrow of the law,
    Setting it up to fear the birds of prey,
    And let it keep one shape, till custom make it
    Their perch, and not their terror.
ESCAL.   Ay, but yet
    Let us be keen, and rather cut a little,
    Than fall, and bruise to death.
    Alas, this gentleman,
    Whom I would save, had a most noble father!
    Let but your honour know,[1]
    Whom I believe to be most strait in virtue,
    That, in the working of your own affections,
    Had time cohered with place or place with wishing,
    Or that the resolute acting of your blood
    Could have attain'd the effect of your own purpose,
    Whether you had not sometime in your life
    Err'd in this point which now you censure him,
    And pull'd the law upon you.
ANG.   'T is one thing to be tempted, Escalus,
    Another thing to fall. I not deny,
    The jury, passing on the prisoner's life,
    May in the sworn twelve have a thief or two
    Guiltier than him they try. What's open made to justice,
    That justice seizes: what know the laws

---

[1] *know*] examine, consider, take cognizance of. The word is used in the same sense by Angelo, below: "what *know* the laws," etc., *i.e.*, "What cognizance can the laws take of the circumstance that thieves may possibly pass judgment on thieves?"

That thieves do pass on thieves? 'T is very pregnant,
The jewel that we find, we stoop and take 't,
Because we see it; but what we do not see
We tread upon, and never think of it.
You may not so extenuate his offence
For[2] I have had such faults; but rather tell me,
When I, that censure him, do so offend,
Let mine own judgement pattern out my death,
And nothing come in partial.[3] Sir, he must die.

ESCAL.   Be it as your wisdom will.
ANG.   Where is the provost?
PROV.   Here, if it like your honour.
ANG.   See that Claudio
Be executed by nine to-morrow morning:
Bring him his confessor, let him be prepared;
For that's the utmost of his pilgrimage.   [*Exit* PROVOST.
ESCAL.   [*Aside*] Well, heaven forgive him! and forgive us all!
Some rise by sin, and some by virtue fall:
Some run from brakes of ice, and answer none;[4]
And some condemned for a fault alone.

Enter ELBOW, *and* Officers *with* FROTH *and* POMPEY

ELB.   Come, bring them away: if these be good people in a common-
weal that do nothing but use their abuses in common houses, I
know no law: bring them away.
ANG.   How now, sir! What's your name? and what's the matter?
ELB.   If it please your honour, I am the poor Duke's constable, and
my name is Elbow: I do lean upon justice, sir, and do bring in
here before your good honour two notorious benefactors.
ANG.   Benefactors? Well; what benefactors are they? are they not
malefactors?
ELB.   If it please your honour, I know not well what they are: but precise villains they are, that I am sure of; and void of all profanation
in the world that good Christians ought to have.
ESCAL.   This comes off well;[5] here's a wise officer.

---

[2]*For*] For the reason that, because.
[3]*nothing come in partial*] no partiality intervene.
[4]*Some run . . . none*] This is the original reading, and is not easily explained. "Brake" is
variously used for "thicket," "bridle," "trap," and other forms of entanglement. Rowe
and many succeeding editors substitute *vice* for *ice*, and understand by "brakes of vice"
traps or entanglements of sin, which gives the sense required by the context more ob-
viously than the original reading.
[5]*This comes off well*] This is eloquently spoken.

ANG.   Go to: what quality are they of? Elbow is your name? why dost
       thou not speak, Elbow?

POM.   He cannot, sir; he's out at elbow.

ANG.   What are you, sir?

ELB.   He, sir! a tapster, sir; parcel-bawd;[6] one that serves a bad woman;
       whose house, sir, was, as they say, plucked down in the suburbs;
       and now she professes a hot-house,[7] which, I think, is a very ill
       house too.

ESCAL.   How know you that?

ELB.   My wife, sir, whom I detest[8] before heaven and your honour,—

ESCAL.   How? thy wife?

ELB.   Ay, sir;—whom, I thank heaven, is an honest woman,—

ESCAL.   Dost thou detest her therefore?

ELB.   I say, sir, I will detest myself also, as well as she, that this house,
       if it be not a bawd's house, it is pity of her life, for it is a naughty
       house.

ESCAL.   How dost thou know that, constable?

ELB.   Marry, sir, by my wife; who, if she had been a woman cardinally
       given, might have been accused in fornication, adultery, and all
       uncleanliness there.

ESCAL.   By the woman's means?

ELB.   Ay, sir, by Mistress Overdone's means: but as she spit in his face,
       so she defied him.

POM.   Sir, if it please your honour, this is not so.

ELB.   Prove it before these varlets here, thou honourable man; prove
       it.

ESCAL.   Do you hear how he misplaces?

POM.   Sir, she came in great with child; and longing, saving your
       honour's reverence, for stewed prunes;[9] sir, we had but two in the
       house, which at that very distant[10] time stood, as it were, in a fruit-
       dish, a dish of some three-pence; your honours have seen such
       dishes; they are not China dishes, but very good dishes,—

ESCAL.   Go to, go to: no matter for the dish, sir.

POM.   No, indeed, sir, not of a pin; you are therein in the right: but to
       the point. As I say, this Mistress Elbow, being, as I say, with child,
       and being great-bellied, and longing, as I said, for prunes; and

---

[6]*parcel-bawd*] "Parcel" for "part" is frequently used in this sort of combination. Cf. 2
Hen. IV, II, i, 84, "*parcel*-gilt."

[7]*she professes . . . hot-house*] she pretends to keep a bathing establishment.

[8]*detest*] Mrs. Quickly in *M. Wives*, I, iv, 135, also blunderingly uses "detest" for
"protest" or "attest."

[9]*stewed prunes*] a dish invariably provided in brothels, according to ample testimony of
Elizabethan writers.

[10]*distant*] blunder for "instant."

having but two in the dish, as I said, Master Froth here, this very man, having eaten the rest, as I said, and, as I say, paying for them very honestly; for, as you know, Master Froth, I could not give you three-pence again.

FROTH. No, indeed.

POM. Very well;—you being then, if you be remembered, cracking the stones of the foresaid prunes,—

FROTH. Ay, so I did indeed.

POM. Why, very well; I telling you then, if you be remembered, that such a one and such a one were past cure of the thing you wot of, unless they kept very good diet, as I told you,—

FROTH. All this is true.

POM. Why, very well, then,—

ESCAL. Come, you are a tedious fool: to the purpose. What was done to Elbow's wife, that he hath cause to complain of? Come me to what was done to her.

POM. Sir, your honour cannot come to that yet.

ESCAL. No, sir, nor I mean it not.

POM. Sir, but you shall come to it, by your honour's leave. And, I beseech you, look into Master Froth here, sir; a man of fourscore pound a year; whose father died at Hallowmas:—was 't not at Hallowmas, Master Froth?—

FROTH. All-hallond eve.

POM. Why, very well; I hope here be truths. He, sir, sitting, as I say, in a lower chair,[11] sir; 't was in the Bunch of Grapes,[12] where, indeed, you have a delight to sit, have you not?

FROTH. I have so; because it is an open room, and good for winter.[13]

POM. Why, very well, then; I hope here be truths.

ANG. This will last out a night in Russia,
When nights are longest there: I'll take my leave,
And leave you to the hearing of the cause;
Hoping you'll find good cause to whip them all.

ESCAL. I think no less. Good morrow to your lordship.

[*Exit* ANGELO.

Now, sir, come on: what was done to Elbow's wife, once more?

POM. Once, sir? there was nothing done to her once.

ELB. I beseech you, sir, ask him what this man did to my wife.

---

[11]*a lower chair*] a low or easy chair.

[12]*Bunch of Grapes*] The name given to a specific room in the tavern. In *1 Hen. IV*, II, iv, 26, 35, mention is made of rooms in the Boar's-Head tavern termed respectively "Half-moon" and "Pomgarnet," *i.e.* Pomegranate.

[13]*an open room . . . winter*] Possibly a pointless remark on the part of Froth, who is described in the original *dramatis personæ* as "a foolish gentleman." An "open" room is one open either to the public or to the sun.

POM.   I beseech your honour, ask me.

ESCAL.   Well, sir; what did this gentleman to her?

POM.   I beseech you, sir, look in this gentleman's face. Good Master
Froth, look upon his honour; 't is for a good purpose. Doth your
honour mark his face?

ESCAL.   Ay, sir, very well.

POM.   Nay, I beseech you, mark it well.

ESCAL.   Well, I do so.

POM.   Doth your honour see any harm in his face?

ESCAL.   Why, no.

POM.   I'll be supposed[14] upon a book, his face is the worst thing about
him. Good, then; if his face be the worst thing about him, how
could Master Froth do the constable's wife any harm? I would
know that of your honour.

ESCAL.   He's in the right. Constable, what say you to it?

ELB.   First, an it like you, the house is a respected house; next, this is
a respected fellow; and his mistress is a respected woman.

POM.   By this hand, sir, his wife is a more respected person than any
of us all.

ELB.   Varlet, thou liest; thou liest, wicked varlet! the time is yet to
come that she was ever respected with man, woman, or child.

POM.   Sir, she was respected with him before he married with her.

ESCAL.   Which is the wiser here? Justice or Iniquity?[15] Is this true?

ELB.   O thou caitiff! O thou varlet! O thou wicked Hannibal! I respected with her before I was married to her! If ever I was respected with her, or she with me, let not your worship think me
the poor Duke's officer. Prove this, thou wicked Hannibal,[16] or I'll
have mine action of battery on thee.

ESCAL.   If he took you a box o' th' ear, you might have your action of
slander too.

ELB.   Marry, I thank your good worship for it. What is 't your worship's
pleasure I shall do with this wicked caitiff?

ESCAL.   Truly, officer, because he hath some offences in him that
thou wouldst discover if thou couldst, let him continue in his
courses till thou knowest what they are.

ELB.   Marry, I thank your worship for it. Thou seest, thou wicked

---

[14]*supposed*] blunder for "deposed," *i.e.*, "sworn."

[15]*Justice or Iniquity*] Constable or Pompey, the accuser or the accused. In the old morality plays, "Iniquity" was often the name formally conferred on the "Vice" or villain of
the piece. Cf. *1 Hen. IV*, II, iv, 438, "that reverend *vice*, that grey *iniquity*," and *Rich.
III*, III, iv, 82, "thus like the *formal vice, Iniquity*."

[16]*Hannibal*] Blunder for "Cannibal." Cf. *2 Hen. IV*, II, iv, 157, where Pistol makes the
reverse error, and speaks of "Cannibals" for "Hannibals."

varlet, now, what's come upon thee: thou art to continue now, thou varlet; thou art to continue.

ESCAL.   Where were you born, friend?

FROTH.   Here in Vienna, sir.

ESCAL.   Are you of fourscore pounds a year?

FROTH.   Yes, an 't please you, sir.

ESCAL.   So. What trade are you of, sir?

POM.   A tapster; a poor widow's tapster.

ESCAL.   Your mistress' name?

POM.   Mistress Overdone.

ESCAL.   Hath she had any more than one husband?

POM.   Nine, sir; Overdone by the last.

ESCAL.   Nine! Come hither to me, Master Froth. Master Froth, I would not have you acquainted with tapsters: they will draw you, Master Froth, and you will hang[17] them. Get you gone, and let me hear no more of you.

FROTH.   I thank your worship. For mine own part, I never come into any room in a taphouse, but I am drawn in.

ESCAL.   Well, no more of it, Master Froth: farewell. [*Exit* FROTH.] Come you hither to me, Master tapster. What's your name, Master tapster?

POM.   Pompey.

ESCAL.   What else?

POM.   Bum, sir.

ESCAL.   Troth, and your bum is the greatest thing[18] about you; so that, in the beastliest sense, you are Pompey the Great. Pompey, you are partly a bawd, Pompey, howsoever you colour it in being a tapster, are you not? come, tell me true: it shall be the better for you.

POM.   Truly, sir, I am a poor fellow that would live.

ESCAL.   How would you live, Pompey? by being a bawd? What do you think of the trade, Pompey? is it a lawful trade?

POM.   If the law would allow it, sir.

ESCAL.   But the law will not allow it, Pompey; nor it shall not be allowed in Vienna.

POM.   Does your worship mean to geld and splay all the youth of the city?

ESCAL.   No, Pompey.

---

[17]*they will draw you . . . hang*] A pun on varied senses of "draw," *i.e.*, "draw ale," "drain or empty a glass," and "draw a convict to and from the scaffold on the hurdle." "Hang" means here "cause to be hanged," "be the means of hanging (them)."

[18]*the greatest thing*] A jesting allusion to the enormously wide and unsightly trunk-hose worn by Elizabethan gentlemen.

POM.   Truly, sir, in my poor opinion, they will to 't, then. If your worship will take order for the drabs[19] and the knaves, you need not to fear the bawds.

ESCAL.   There are pretty orders beginning, I can tell you: it is but heading and hanging.

POM.   If you head and hang all that offend that way but for ten year together, you'll be glad to give out a commission for more heads: if this law hold in Vienna ten year, I'll rent the fairest house in it after three-pence a bay:[20] if you live to see this come to pass, say Pompey told you so.

ESCAL.   Thank you, good Pompey; and, in requital of your prophecy, hark you: I advise you, let me not find you before me again upon any complaint whatsoever; no, not for dwelling where you do: if I do, Pompey, I shall beat you to your tent, and prove a shrewd Cæsar to you; in plain dealing, Pompey, I shall have you whipt: so, for this time, Pompey, fare you well.

POM.   I thank your worship for your good counsel: [*Aside*] but I shall follow it as the flesh and fortune shall better determine.
Whip me? No, no; let carman whip his jade:
The valiant heart's not whipt out of his trade.   [*Exit.*

ESCAL.   Come hither to me, Master Elbow; come hither, Master constable. How long have you been in this place of constable?

ELB.   Seven year and a half, sir.

ESCAL.   I thought, by your readiness[21] in the office, you had continued in it some time. You say, seven years together?

ELB.   And a half, sir.

ESCAL.   Alas, it hath been great pains to you. They do you wrong to put you so oft upon 't: are there not men in your ward sufficient to serve it?

ELB.   Faith, sir, few of any wit in such matters: as they are chosen, they are glad to choose me for them; I do it for some piece of money, and go through with all.

ESCAL.   Look you bring me in the names of some six or seven, the most sufficient of your parish.

ELB.   To your worship's house, sir?

ESCAL.   To my house. Fare you well.   [*Exit* ELBOW.
What's o'clock, think you?

JUST.   Eleven, sir.

---

[19]*take order . . . drabs*] take measures for dealing with the loose women.
[20]*three-pence a bay*] A "bay" seems to have been a recognized standard in the measurement of houses, each bay being about twenty feet in length. "After" here means "at the rate of."
[21]*your readiness*] Pope's emendation of the original reading *the readiness*.

ESCAL.   I pray you home to dinner with me.
JUST.   I humbly thank you.
ESCAL.   It grieves me for the death of Claudio;
    But there's no remedy.
JUST.   Lord Angelo is severe.
ESCAL.   It is but needful:
    Mercy is not itself, that oft looks so;
    Pardon is still the nurse of second woe:
    But yet,—poor Claudio! There is no remedy.
    Come, sir.   [*Exeunt.*

SCENE II. *Another Room in the Same.*

Enter PROVOST *and a* Servant

SERV.   He's hearing of a cause; he will come straight: I'll tell him of
    you.
PROV.   Pray you do. [*Exit* Servant.] I'll know
    His pleasure; may be he will relent. Alas,
    He hath but as offended in a dream!
    All sects, all ages smack of this vice; and he
    To die for 't!

Enter ANGELO

ANG.   Now, what's the matter, provost?
PROV.   Is it your will Claudio shall die to-morrow?
ANG.   Did not I tell thee yea? hadst thou not order?
    Why dost thou ask again?
PROV.   Lest I might be too rash:
    Under your good correction, I have seen,
    When, after execution, Judgement hath
    Repented o'er his doom.
ANG.   Go to; let that be mine:
    Do you your office, or give up your place,
    And you shall well be spared.
PROV.   I crave your honour's pardon.
    What shall be done, sir, with the groaning Juliet?
    She's very near her hour.
ANG.   Dispose of her
    To some more fitter place, and that with speed.

Re-enter Servant

SERV.   Here is the sister of the man condemn'd

Desires access to you.

ANG.   Hath he a sister?

PROV. Ay, my good lord; a very virtuous maid,
     And to be shortly of a sisterhood,
     If not already.

ANG.   Well, let her be admitted.   [*Exit* Servant.
     See you the fornicatress be removed:
     Let her have needful, but not lavish, means;
     There shall be order for 't.

Enter ISABELLA *and* LUCIO

PROV.   God save your honour!

ANG. Stay a little while. [*To* ISAB.] You're welcome: what's your will?

ISAB. I am a woeful suitor to your honour,
     Please but your honour hear me.

ANG.   Well; what's your suit?

ISAB. There is a vice that most I do abhor,
     And most desire should meet the blow of justice;
     For which I would not plead, but that I must;
     For which I must not plead, but that I am
     At war 'twixt will and will not.

ANG.   Well; the matter?

ISAB. I have a brother is condemn'd to die:
     I do beseech you, let it be his fault,
     And not my brother.

PROV. [*Aside*]   Heaven give thee moving graces!

ANG. Condemn the fault, and not the actor of it?
     Why, every fault's condemn'd ere it be done:
     Mine were the very cipher of a function,
     To fine the faults whose fine stands in record,[1]
     And let go by the actor.

ISAB.   O just but severe law!
     I had a brother, then.—Heaven keep your honour!

LUCIO. [*Aside to* ISAB.] Give 't not o'er so: to him again, entreat him;
     Kneel down before him, hang upon his gown:
     You are too cold; if you should need a pin,
     You could not with more tame a tongue desire it:
     To him, I say!

ISAB. Must he needs die?

ANG.   Maiden, no remedy.

ISAB. Yes; I do think that you might pardon him,

---

[1]*To fine . . . record*] To adjudge punishment for the fault, penalty for which is duly prescribed.

And neither heaven nor man grieve at the mercy.

ANG.   I will not do 't.

ISAB.   But can you, if you would?

ANG.   Look, what I will not, that I cannot do.

ISAB.   But might you do 't, and do the world no wrong,
> If so your heart were touch'd with that remorse
> As mine is to him?

ANG.   He's sentenced; 't is too late.

LUCIO.   [*Aside to* ISAB.] You are too cold.

ISAB.   Too late? why, no; I, that do speak a word,
> May call it back again. Well, believe this,
> No ceremony that to great ones 'longs,
> Not the king's crown, nor the deputed sword,
> The marshal's truncheon, nor the judge's robe,
> Become them with one half so good a grace
> As mercy does.
> If he had been as you, and you as he,
> You would have slipt like him; but he, like you,
> Would not have been so stern.

ANG.   Pray you, be gone.

ISAB.   I would to heaven I had your potency,
> And you were Isabel! should it then be thus?
> No; I would tell what 't were to be a judge,
> And what a prisoner.

LUCIO.   [*Aside to* ISAB.] Ay, touch him; there's the vein.

ANG.   Your brother is a forfeit of the law,
> And you but waste your words.

ISAB.   Alas, alas!
> Why, all the souls that were were forfeit once;
> And He that might the vantage best have took
> Found out the remedy. How would you be,
> If He, which is the top of judgement,[2] should
> But judge you as you are? O, think on that;
> And mercy then will breathe within your lips,
> Like man new made.[3]

ANG.   Be you content, fair maid;
> It is the law, not I condemn your brother:
> Were he my kinsman, brother, or my son,
> It should be thus with him: he must die to-morrow.

---

[2] *top of judgement*] Dante uses precisely the same phrase: "Cima di giudicio," *Purg.*,
673.

[3] *Like man new made*] Like man regenerated, in the scriptural sense. Cf. John iii, v. 3–8:
"Except a man be born again," etc.

ISAB.   To-morrow! O, that's sudden! Spare him, spare him!
    He's not prepared for death. Even for our kitchens
    We kill the fowl of season:[4] shall we serve heaven
    With less respect than we do minister
    To our gross selves? Good, good my lord, bethink you;
    Who is it that hath died for this offence?
    There's many have committed it.
LUCIO.   [*Aside to* ISAB.] Ay, well said.
ANG.   The law hath not been dead, though it hath slept:
    Those many had not dared to do that evil,
    If the first[5] that did the edict infringe
    Had answer'd for his deed: now 't is awake,
    Takes note of what is done; and, like a prophet,
    Looks in a glass,[6] that shows what future evils,
    Either now, or by remissness new-conceived,
    And so in progress to be hatch'd and born,
    Are now to have no successive degrees,
    But, ere they live, to end.
ISAB.   Yet show some pity.
ANG.   I show it most of all when I show justice;
    For then I pity those I do not know,
    Which a dismiss'd offence would after gall;[7]
    And do him right that, answering one foul wrong,
    Lives not to act another. Be satisfied;
    Your brother dies to-morrow; be content.
ISAB.   So you must be the first that gives this sentence,
    And he, that suffers. O, it is excellent
    To have a giant's strength; but it is tyrannous
    To use it like a giant.
LUCIO.   [*Aside to* ISAB.] That's well said.
ISAB.   Could great men thunder
    As Jove himself does, Jove would ne'er be quiet,
    For every pelting, petty officer
    Would use his heaven for thunder.
    Nothing but thunder! Merciful Heaven,
    Thou rather with thy sharp and sulphurous bolt
    Split'st the unwedgeable and gnarled oak

---

[4]*fowl of season*] a fowl when fit for killing, at the right season.
[5]*If the first, etc.*] The meter seems to require some such change as *If he the first* or *If the first man.*
[6]*glass*] magic crystal.
[7]*Which a dismiss'd . . . gall*] Whom the dismissal or dropping of the charge would cause subsequent irritation.

Than the soft myrtle: but man, proud man,
Drest in a little brief authority,
Most ignorant of what he's most assured,
His glassy essence,[8] like an angry ape,
Plays such fantastic tricks before high heaven
As make the angels weep; who, with our spleens,
Would all themselves laugh mortal.[9]

LUCIO. [*Aside to* ISAB.] O, to him, to him, wench! he will relent;
He's coming; I perceive 't.

PROV.   [*Aside*] Pray heaven she wins him!

ISAB. We cannot weigh our brother with ourself:[10]
Great men may jest with saints; 't is wit in them,
But in the less foul profanation.

LUCIO. Thou'rt i' the right, girl; more o' that.

ISAB. That in the captain's but a choleric word,
Which in the soldier is flat blasphemy.

LUCIO. [*Aside to* ISAB.] Art avised o' that?[11] more on 't.

ANG. Why do you put these sayings upon me?

ISAB. Because authority, though it err like others,
Hath yet a kind of medicine in itself,
That skins the vice[12] o' the top. Go to your bosom;
Knock there, and ask your heart what it doth know
That's like my brother's fault: if it confess
A natural guiltiness such as is his,
Let it not sound a thought upon your tongue
Against my brother's life.

ANG.   [*Aside*] She speaks, and 't is
Such sense, that my sense breeds with it.[13] Fare you well.

ISAB. Gentle my lord, turn back.

ANG. I will bethink me: come again to-morrow.

ISAB. Hark how I'll bribe you: good my lord, turn back.

ANG. How? bribe me?

ISAB. Ay, with such gifts that heaven shall share with you.

LUCIO. [*Aside to* ISAB.] You had marr'd all else.

---

[8]*His glassy essence*] His brittle being.

[9]*who . . . mortal*] who, with human capacity for mirth, would all laugh till they died, laugh themselves out of their immortality, never do anything but laugh.

[10]*weigh . . . with ourself*] One cannot treat one's neighbor as on precisely the same level with one's self; we are not all of the same scale.

[11]*Art avised o' that?*] Are you sure of that?

[12]*skins the vice*] covers with a skin. Cf. *Hamlet*, III, iv, 147: "It [*i.e.*, that flattering unction] will but *skin and film* the ulcerous place."

[13]*my sense breeds with it*] my sensual desire is generated, excited by what she says, by her reasonableness.

ISAB.   Not with fond sicles[14] of the tested gold,
        Or stones whose rates are either rich or poor
        As fancy values them; but with true prayers
        That shall be up at heaven and enter there
        Ere sun-rise, prayers from preserved souls,
        From fasting maids whose minds are dedicate
        To nothing temporal.
ANG.   Well; come to me to-morrow.
LUCIO.   [*Aside to* ISAB.] Go to; 't is well; away!
ISAB.   Heaven keep your honour safe!
ANG.   [*Aside*] Amen:
        For I am that way going to temptation,
        Where prayers cross.[15]
ISAB.   At what hour to-morrow
        Shall I attend your lordship?
ANG.   At any time 'fore noon.
ISAB.   'Save your honour!

                        [*Exeunt* ISABELLA, LUCIO, *and* PROVOST.
ANG.   From thee,—even from thy virtue!
        What's this, what's this? Is this her fault or mine?
        The tempter or the tempted, who sins most?
        Ha!
        Not she; nor doth she tempt: but it is I
        That, lying by the violet in the sun,
        Do as the carrion does, not as the flower,
        Corrupt with virtuous season.[16] Can it be
        That modesty may more betray our sense[17]
        Than woman's lightness? Having waste ground enough,
        Shall we desire to raze the sanctuary,
        And pitch our evils[18] there? O, fie, fie, fie!
        What dost thou, or what art thou, Angelo?
        Dost thou desire her foully for those things
        That make her good? O, let her brother live:
        Thieves for their robbery have authority

---

[14]*sicles*] The Folio reading is *sickles*, which Pope altered to *shekels*. No doubt "shekels"
   is what is meant. In the translation of the Bible known as "The Bishop's Bible," which
   was the authorized version of Elizabeth's reign, the word is spelled "sicles."
[15]*cross*] hinder, in the way.
[16]*I . . . season*] Unlike the violet, the flower which flourishes in the summer sun, I, like
   carrion, grow putrid in the sunlight, in the season that should encourage healthy
   growth.
[17]*sense*] sensual desire.
[18]*evils*] doubtfully explained as "privies." The word may merely be used for "evil, un-
   sanctified deeds."

When judges steal themselves. What, do I love her,
That I desire to hear her speak again,
And feast upon her eyes? What is 't I dream on?
O cunning enemy, that, to catch a saint,
With saints dost bait thy hook! Most dangerous
Is that temptation that doth goad us on
To sin in loving virtue: never could the strumpet,
With all her double vigour, art and nature,
Once stir my temper; but this virtuous maid
Subdues me quite. Ever till now,
When men were fond, I smiled, and wonder'd how.   [*Exit.*

SCENE III. *A Room in a Prison.*

Enter, severally, DUKE *disguised as a friar, and* PROVOST

DUKE.   Hail to you, provost! so I think you are.
PROV.   I am the provost. What's your will, good friar?
DUKE.   Bound by my charity and my blest order,
    I come to visit the afflicted spirits
    Here in the prison. Do me the common right
    To let me see them, and to make me know
    The nature of their crimes, that I may minister
    To them accordingly.
PROV.   I would do more than that, if more were needful.

Enter JULIET

    Look, here comes one: a gentlewoman of mine,
    Who, falling in the flaws of her own youth,[1]
    Hath blister'd her report: she is with child;
    And he that got it, sentenced; a young man
    More fit to do another such offence
    Than die for this.
DUKE.   When must he die?
PROV.   As I do think, to-morrow.
    I have provided for you: stay awhile,   [*To* JULIET.
    And you shall be conducted.
DUKE.   Repent you, fair one, of the sin you carry?
JUL.   I do; and bear the shame most patiently.

---

[1]*flaws of her own youth*] *Flaws*, the original reading, was altered by D'Avenant to *flames*,
with which "blister'd" in the next line undoubtedly harmonizes, but the change here
is not essential. "Blister'd her report" merely means "disfigured her fame."

DUKE.   I'll teach you how you shall arraign your conscience,
    And try your penitence, if it be sound,
    Or hollowly put on.
JUL.   I'll gladly learn.
DUKE.   Love you the man that wrong'd you?
JUL.   Yes, as I love the woman that wrong'd him.
DUKE.   So, then, it seems your most offenceful act
    Was mutually committed?
JUL.   Mutually.
DUKE.   Then was your sin of heavier kind than his.
JUL.   I do confess it, and repent it, father.
DUKE.   'T is meet so, daughter: but lest you do repent,
    As that the sin hath brought you to this shame,
    Which sorrow is always toward ourselves, not heaven,
    Showing we would not spare heaven as we love it,
    But as we stand in fear,[2]—
JUL.   I do repent me, as it is an evil,
    And take the shame with joy.
DUKE.   There rest.
    Your partner, as I hear, must die to-morrow,
    And I am going with instruction to him.
    Grace go with you, *Benedicite!*   [*Exit.*
JUL.   Must die to-morrow! O injurious love,[3]
    That respites me a life, whose very comfort
    Is still a dying horror!
PROV.   'T is pity of him.   [*Exeunt.*

SCENE IV. *A Room in Angelo's House.*

Enter ANGELO

ANG.   When I would pray and think, I think and pray
    To several subjects. Heaven hath my empty words;
    Whilst my invention, hearing not my tongue,
    Anchors on Isabel: Heaven in my mouth,
    As if I did but only chew his name;
    And in my heart the strong and swelling evil

[2]*lest . . . stand in fear*] The speech is unfinished, because Juliet interrupts. The Duke
bids the girl beware lest her repentance is merely because her sin has brought her to
shame. Such sorrow is a selfish sense of personal disgrace, not a consciousness of an
offense against God.
[3]*love*] Hanmer substituted *law*, but the original reading, *love*, probably means here indulgence or kindness.

Of my conception. The state, whereon I studied,
Is like a good thing, being often read,
Grown fear'd[1] and tedious; yea, my gravity,
Wherein—let no man hear me—I take pride,
Could I with boot change for an idle plume,
Which the air beats for vain.[2] O place, O form,
How often dost thou with thy case, thy habit,
Wrench awe from fools, and tie the wiser souls
To thy false seeming! Blood, thou art blood:
Let's write good angel on the devil's horn;
'T is not the devil's crest.[3]

Enter a Servant

                        How now! who's there?
SERV.   One Isabel, a sister, desires access to you.
ANG.   Teach her the way. O heavens!
Why does my blood thus muster to my heart,
Making both it unable for itself,
And dispossessing all my other parts
Of necessary fitness?
So play the foolish throngs with one that swoons;
Come all to help him, and so stop the air
By which he should revive: and even so
The general[4] subject to a well-wish'd king
Quit their own part, and in obsequious fondness
Crowd to his presence, where their untaught love
Must needs appear offence.

Enter ISABELLA

                        How now, fair maid?
ISAB.   I am come to know your pleasure.
ANG.   That you might know it, would much better please me
Than to demand what 't is. Your brother cannot live.
ISAB.   Even so.—Heaven keep your honour!
ANG.   Yet may he live awhile; and, it may be,
As long as you or I: yet he must die.
ISAB.   Under your sentence?
ANG.   Yea.

[1]*fear'd*] approached with fear or reluctance, dreaded. The commonly substituted *sear'd* is unnecessary.
[2]*with boot . . . for vain*] with advantage . . . in vain, idly.
[3]*Let's write . . . crest*] You may inscribe an innocent legend on the devil's horn, but you won't make innocence the genuine motto of the devil.
[4]*The general*] The crowd, as in *Hamlet*, II, ii, 430: "caviare to *the general*."

ISAB.   When, I beseech you? that in his reprieve,
   Longer or shorter, he may be so fitted[5]
   That his soul sicken not.

ANG.   Ha! fie, these filthy vices! It were as good
   To pardon him that hath from nature stolen
   A man already made, as to remit
   Their saucy sweetness that do coin heaven's image
   In stamps that are forbid:[6] 't is all as easy
   Falsely to take away a life true made,
   As to put metal in restrained means[7]
   To make a false one.

ISAB.   'T is set down so in heaven, but not in earth.

ANG.   Say you so? then I shall pose you quickly.
   Which had you rather,—that the most just law
   Now took your brother's life; or, to redeem him,
   Give up your body to such sweet uncleanness[8]
   As she that he hath stain'd?

ISAB.   Sir, believe this,
   I had rather give my body than my soul.

ANG.   I talk not of your soul: our compell'd sins
   Stand more for number than for accompt.[9]

ISAB.   How say you?

ANG.   Nay, I'll not warrant that; for I can speak
   Against the thing I say. Answer to this:—
   I, now the voice of the recorded law,
   Pronounce a sentence on your brother's life:
   Might there not be a charity in sin
   To save this brother's life?

ISAB.   Please you to do 't,
   I'll take it as a peril to my soul,
   It is no sin at all, but charity.

ANG.   Pleased you to do 't at peril of your soul,
   Were equal poise of sin and charity.

ISAB.   That I do beg his life, if it be sin,

---

[5] *so fitted*] so furnished, so prepared (with religious counsel).
[6] *It were . . . forbid*] It were as right to pardon a murder as to pardon the wanton indulgence in the sweet sin of fornication. The metaphor of coinage in this connection is very common. Cf. *Edward III* (1596), II, i, 258: "To *stamp* his [*i.e.*, the king of heaven's] *image in forbidden metal*," and *Cymb.*, II, v, 5: "When I was *stamped*, some *coiner* with his tools Made me a *counterfeit*."
[7] *in restrained means*] after forbidden methods.
[8] *sweet uncleanness*] the sin of fornication.
[9] *our compell'd sins . . . accompt*] Sinful acts, to which we are forced by violence, are ciphered up but are not entered in the account for which we are held liable.

　　　Heaven let me bear it! you granting of my suit,
　　　If that be sin, I'll make it my morn prayer
　　　To have it added to the faults of mine,
　　　And nothing of your answer.[10]

ANG.　　　　　　　　　　　　Nay, but hear me.
　　　Your sense pursues not mine: either you are ignorant,
　　　Or seem so, craftily; and that's not good.

ISAB.　Let me be ignorant, and in nothing good,
　　　But graciously to know I am no better.

ANG.　Thus wisdom wishes to appear most bright
　　　When it doth tax itself; as these black masks
　　　Proclaim an enshield beauty[11] ten times louder
　　　Than beauty could, display'd. But mark me;
　　　To be received plain, I'll speak more gross:
　　　Your brother is to die.

ISAB.　So.

ANG.　And his offence is so, as it appears,
　　　Accountant to the law upon that pain.[12]

ISAB.　True.

ANG.　Admit no other way to save his life,—
　　　As I subscribe not that, nor any other,
　　　But in the loss of question,[13]—that you, his sister,
　　　Finding yourself desired of such a person,
　　　Whose credit with the judge, or own great place,
　　　Could fetch your brother from the manacles
　　　Of the all-building law;[14] and that there were
　　　No earthly mean to save him, but that either
　　　You must lay down the treasures of your body
　　　To this supposed, or else to let him suffer;
　　　What would you do?

ISAB.　As much for my poor brother as myself:
　　　That is, were I under the terms of death,
　　　The impression of keen whips I 'ld wear as rubies,
　　　And strip myself to death, as to a bed

---

[10]*nothing of your answer*] nothing for which you should be made responsible.

[11]*Proclaim an enshield beauty*] The general meaning is: beauty that hides behind black masks excites more public notice or expectation than beauty that is openly displayed. Cf. *Rom. and Jul.* I, i, 236–237: "These happy masks that kiss fair ladies' brows, Being black, put us in mind they hide the fair."

[12]*that pain*] the prescribed penalty, punishment.

[13]*in the loss of question*] in idle talk, in the waste of words for the sake of argument.

[14]*all-building law*] law on which everything is built, law which is the foundation of everything. Dr. Johnson substituted *all-binding*, but the original reading is more pointed.

That longing have been[15] sick for, ere I 'ld yield
My body up to shame.

ANG.   Then must your brother die.

ISAB.   And 't were the cheaper way:
Better it were a brother died at once,
Than that a sister, by redeeming him,
Should die for ever.

ANG.   Were not you, then, as cruel as the sentence
That you have slander'd so?

ISAB.   Ignomy[16] in ransom and free pardon
Are of two houses: lawful mercy
Is nothing kin to foul redemption.

ANG.   You seem'd of late to make the law a tyrant;
And rather proved the sliding of your brother
A merriment than a vice.

ISAB.   O, pardon me, my lord; it oft falls out,
To have what we would have, we speak not what we mean:
I something do excuse the thing I hate,
For his advantage that I dearly love.

ANG.   We are all frail.

ISAB.   Else let my brother die,
If not a feodary, but only he
Owe and succeed thy weakness.[17]

ANG.   Nay, women are frail too.

ISAB.   Ay, as the glasses where they view themselves;
Which are as easy broke as they make forms.
Women!—Help Heaven! men their creation mar
In profiting by them.[18] Nay, call us ten times frail;
For we are soft as our complexions are,
And credulous to false prints.[19]

ANG.   I think it well:
And from this testimony of your own sex,—
Since, I suppose, we are made to be no stronger

---

[15]*longing have been*] "I" is here implied to govern "have been." Such an ellipse is rare.

[16]*Ignomy*] A common abbreviation of ignominy. Cf. *Troil. and Cress.*, V, x, 33: "ignomy and shame."

[17]*If not a feodary . . . weakness*] I would let my brother die, if he had no "feodary" (*i.e.*, associate) in his sin; if he alone owned and followed the weakness that you admit.

[18]*men . . . by them*] men debase their nature by taking advantage of these weak creatures.

[19]*credulous to false prints*] apt to trust falsehood, prone to receive counterfeited impressions. Cf. *Tw. Night*, II, ii, 30–31: "How easy is it for the proper-*false* In women's *waxen* hearts to *set* their *forms*!"

    Than faults[20] may shake our frames,—let me be bold;—
    I do arrest your words. Be that you are,
    That is, a woman; if you be more, you're none;
    If you be one,—as you are well express'd
    By all external warrants,—show it now,
    By putting on the destined livery.

ISAB.   I have no tongue but one: gentle my lord,
    Let me entreat you speak the former language.

ANG.   Plainly conceive, I love you.

ISAB.   My brother did love Juliet,
    And you tell me that he shall die for it.

ANG.   He shall not, Isabel, if you give me love.

ISAB.   I know your virtue hath a license in 't,
    Which seems a little fouler than it is,
    To pluck on others.[21]

ANG.   Believe me, on mine honour,
    My words express my purpose.

ISAB.   Ha! little honour to be much believed,
    And most pernicious purpose!—Seeming, seeming![22]—
    I will proclaim thee, Angelo; look for 't;
    Sign me a present pardon for my brother,
    Or with an outstretch'd throat I'll tell the world aloud
    What man thou art.

ANG.   Who will believe thee, Isabel?
    My unsoil'd name, the austereness of my life,
    My vouch[23] against you, and my place i' the state,
    Will so your accusation overweigh,
    That you shall stifle in your own report,
    And smell of calumny. I have begun;
    And now I give my sensual race[24] the rein:
    Fit thy consent to my sharp appetite;
    Lay by all nicety and prolixious blushes,[25]
    That banish what they sue for; redeem thy brother
    By yielding up thy body to my will;
    Or else he must not only die the death,
    But thy unkindness shall his death draw out

---

[20]*no stronger . . . Than faults . . .*] not so strong but that faults . . .

[21]*your virtue . . . To pluck on others*] Your virtue assumes this tone of licentiousness, which sounds worse than it is, in order to test other people, to draw them into damaging admissions.

[22]*Seeming*] Hypocrisy, counterfeit virtue.

[23]*My vouch*] My declaration, testimony.

[24]*sensual race*] sensual bent, disposition.

[25]*prolixious blushes*] blushes inviting delay.

To lingering sufferance. Answer me to-morrow,
Or, by the affection that now guides me most,
I'll prove a tyrant to him. As for you,
Say what you can, my false o'erweighs your true.   [*Exit.*

ISAB.   To whom should I complain? Did I tell this,
Who would believe me? O perilous mouths,
That bear in them one and the self-same tongue,
Either of condemnation or approof;
Bidding the law make court'sy to their will;
Hooking both right and wrong to the appetite,
To follow as it draws! I'll to my brother:
Though he hath fall'n by prompture of the blood,
Yet hath he in him such a mind of honour,
That, had he twenty heads to tender down
On twenty bloody blocks, he 'ld yield them up,
Before his sister should her body stoop
To such abhorr'd pollution.
Then, Isabel, live chaste, and, brother, die:
More than our brother is our chastity.
I'll tell him yet of Angelo's request,
And fit his mind to death, for his soul's rest.   [*Exit.*

ACT III.

SCENE I. *A Room in the Prison.*

Enter DUKE *disguised as before,* CLAUDIO, *and* PROVOST

DUKE. So, then, you hope of pardon from Lord Angelo?
CLAUD. The miserable have no other medicine
    But only hope:
    I've hope to live, and am prepared to die.
DUKE. Be absolute[1] for death; either death or life
    Shall thereby be the sweeter.
    Reason thus with life:
    If I do lose thee, I do lose a thing
    That none but fools would keep: a breath thou art,
    Servile to all the skyey influences,
    That dost this habitation, where thou keep'st,
    Hourly afflict: merely, thou art death's fool;
    For him thou labour'st by thy flight to shun,
    And yet runn'st toward him still. Thou art not noble;
    For all the accommodations that thou bear'st
    Are nursed by baseness. Thou 'rt by no means valiant;
    For thou dost fear the soft and tender fork
    Of a poor worm.[2] Thy best of rest is sleep,
    And that thou oft provokest; yet grossly fear'st
    Thy death, which is no more. Thou art not thyself;
    For thou exist'st on many a thousand grains
    That issue out of dust. Happy thou art not;
    For what thou hast not, still thou strivest to get,
    And what thou hast, forget'st. Thou art not certain;
    For thy complexion shifts to strange effects,

---

[1]*Be absolute*] Be resolved, make up your mind.
[2]*fork Of a poor worm*] forked tongue of a snake or adder. Cf. *Macbeth*, IV, i, 16, "adder's fork."

    After the moon.[3] If thou art rich, thou 'rt poor;
    For, like an ass whose back with ingots bows,
    Thou bear'st thy heavy riches but a journey,
    And death unloads thee. Friend hast thou none;
    For thine own bowels, which do call thee sire,
    The mere effusion of thy proper loins,
    Do curse the gout, serpigo, and the rheum,
    For ending thee no sooner. Thou hast nor youth nor age,
    But, as it were, an after-dinner's sleep,
    Dreaming on both; for all thy blessed youth
    Becomes as aged, and doth beg the alms
    Of palsied eld;[4] and when thou art old and rich,
    Thou hast neither heat, affection, limb, nor beauty,
    To make thy riches pleasant. What's yet in this
    That bears the name of life? Yet in this life
    Lie hid moe thousand deaths: yet death we fear,
    That makes these odds all even.
CLAUD.   I humbly thank you.
    To sue to live, I find I seek to die;
    And, seeking death, find life: let it come on.
ISAB.   [*within*] What, ho! Peace here; grace and good company!
PROV.   Who's there? come in: the wish deserves a welcome.
DUKE.   Dear sir, ere long I'll visit you again.
CLAUD.   Most holy sir, I thank you.

Enter ISABELLA

ISAB.   My business is a word or two with Claudio.
PROV.   And very welcome. Look, signior, here's your sister.
DUKE.   Provost, a word with you.
PROV.   As many as you please.
DUKE.   Bring me to hear them speak, where I may be concealed.
                                     [*Exeunt* DUKE *and* PROVOST.
CLAUD.   Now, sister, what's the comfort?
ISAB.   Why,
    As all comforts are; most good, most good indeed.[5]
    Lord Angelo, having affairs to heaven,
    Intends you for his swift ambassador,

[3]*thy complexion . . . moon*] thy temperament is liable to strange manifestations of change under the influence of the inconstant moon.
[4]*thy blessed youth . . . eld*] Youth is a prey to the cares of age and begs money of trembling and decrepit old men.
[5]*As all . . . indeed*] The line scans badly, but Isabella's perturbation justifies the irregularity. The sense is improved by the substitution of a comma for the semicolon after "are." Pope and other editors omit the second *most good*.

Where you shall be an everlasting leiger:[6]
Therefore your best appointment[7] make with speed;
To-morrow you set on.

CLAUD.   Is there no remedy?

ISAB.   None, but such remedy as, to save a head,
      To cleave a heart in twain.

CLAUD.   But is there any?

ISAB.   Yes, brother, you may live:
      There is a devilish mercy in the judge,
      If you'll implore it, that will free your life,
      But fetter you till death.

CLAUD.   Perpetual durance?

ISAB.   Ay, just; perpetual durance, a restraint,
      Though all the world's vastidity you had,
      To a determined scope.[8]

CLAUD.   But in what nature?

ISAB.   In such a one as, you consenting to 't,
      Would bark your honour from that trunk you bear,
      And leave you naked.

CLAUD.   Let me know the point.

ISAB.   O, I do fear thee, Claudio; and I quake,
      Lest thou a feverous life shouldst entertain,
      And six or seven winters more respect
      Than a perpetual honour. Darest thou die?
      The sense of death is most in apprehension;
      And the poor beetle, that we tread upon,
      In corporal sufferance finds a pang as great
      As when a giant dies.[9]

CLAUD.   Why give you me this shame?
      Think you I can a resolution fetch
      From flowery tenderness?[10] If I must die,
      I will encounter darkness as a bride,
      And hug it in mine arms.

ISAB.   There spake my brother; there my father's grave

---

[6]*an everlasting leiger*] a permanent resident minister.

[7]*appointment*] preparation for travel, outfit, equipment. Cf. *Hamlet*, I, v, 77, "disap-
pointed" (*i.e.*, unprepared, ill equipped), and in modern usage "a well-*appointed*
household."

[8]*a restraint . . . scope*] a confinement, though you had the vastness of the world to roam
over, within the fixed limits (of shame and remorse).

[9]*As when a giant dies*] A giant feels no greater pang in dying than a beetle; only the ap-
prehension of death is painful.

[10]*Why give me . . . flowery tenderness?*] Why shame me by assuming that I can get
courage out of this florid and gentle philosophizing?

Did utter forth a voice. Yes, thou must die:
Thou art too noble to conserve a life
In base appliances.[11] This outward-sainted deputy,
Whose settled visage and deliberate word
Nips youth i' the head, and follies doth emmew
As falcon doth the fowl,[12] is yet a devil;
His filth within being cast,[13] he would appear
A pond as deep as hell.

CLAUD. The prenzie Angelo![14]

ISAB.   O, 't is the cunning livery of hell,
The damned'st body to invest and cover
In prenzie guards![15] Dost thou think, Claudio?—
If I would yield him my virginity,
Thou mightst be freed.

CLAUD.   O heavens! it cannot be.

ISAB.   Yes, he would give 't thee, from this rank offence
So to offend him still.[16] This night's the time
That I should do what I abhor to name,
Or else thou diest to-morrow.

CLAUD.   Thou shalt not do 't.

ISAB.   O, were it but my life,
I 'ld throw it down for your deliverance
As frankly as a pin.

CLAUD.   Thanks, dear Isabel.

ISAB.   Be ready, Claudio, for your death to-morrow.

CLAUD.   Yes. Has he affections in him,
That thus can make him bite the law by the nose,
When he would force[17] it? Sure, it is no sin;
Or of the deadly seven it is the least.

ISAB.   Which is the least?

CLAUD.   If it were damnable, he being so wise,
Why would he for the momentary trick
Be perdurably fined?—O Isabel!

---

[11]*In base appliances*] In degraded ways.

[12]*follies . . . the fowl*] coops follies up, forces them into cover, like the falcon, which, when it takes wing, forces the timid fowl to hide.

[13]*being cast*] being diagnosed.

[14]*The prenzie Angelo*] Thus the First Folio, for which the Second and later Folios reasonably substitute *princely*, as no such word seems known elsewhere in Elizabethan literature.

[15]*guards*] The ornamental facings or border of a livery or uniform.

[16]*he would give . . . still*] he would give you, as the result of this noisome sin of mine, liberty to commit the offense for which he now condemns you.

[17]*affections . . . force*] passions . . . enforce.

ISAB.   What says my brother?
CLAUD.   Death is a fearful thing.
ISAB.   And shamed life a hateful.
CLAUD.   Ay, but to die, and go we know not where;
    To lie in cold obstruction and to rot;
    This sensible warm motion to become
    A kneaded clod; and the delighted[18] spirit
    To bathe in fiery floods, or to reside
    In thrilling region of thick-ribbed ice;
    To be imprison'd in the viewless winds,
    And blown with restless violence round about
    The pendent world; or to be worse than worst
    Of those that lawless and incertain thought[19]
    Imagine howling:—'t is too horrible!
    The weariest and most loathed worldly life
    That age, ache, penury,[20] and imprisonment
    Can lay on nature is a paradise
    To what we fear of death.
ISAB.   Alas, alas!
CLAUD.   Sweet sister, let me live:
    What sin you do to save a brother's life,
    Nature dispenses with[21] the deed so far
    That it becomes a virtue.
ISAB.   O you beast!
    O faithless coward! O dishonest wretch!
    Wilt thou be made a man out of my vice?
    Is 't not a kind of incest, to take life
    From thine own sister's shame? What should I think?
    Heaven shield[22] my mother play'd my father fair!
    For such a warped slip of wilderness[23]
    Ne'er issued from his blood. Take my defiance!
    Die, perish! Might but my bending down
    Reprieve thee from thy fate, it should proceed:
    I'll pray a thousand prayers for thy death.
    No word to save thee.

[18]*delighted*] accustomed to delight or joy.
[19]*thought*] Thus the Folios. Theobald substituted *thoughts*, making the word the subject of "imagine." This emendation seems reasonable. As the text stands, "those that" must govern "imagine," of which "thought" must be the object.
[20]*penury*] Thus the Second and later Folios. The First Folio has the misprint *periury*.
[21]*dispenses with*] grants dispensation for.
[22]*Heaven shield*] Cf. *All's Well*, I, iii, 159: "*God shield* [*i.e.*, forbid] you mean it not!" "God shield," *i.e.*, "God forbid," is common in Elizabethan authors.
[23]*slip of wilderness*] slip of wildness, wild cub.

CLAUD.   Nay, hear me, Isabel.
ISAB.   O, fie, fie, fie!
    Thy sin 's not accidental, but a trade.
    Mercy to thee would prove itself a bawd:
    'T is best that thou diest quickly.
CLAUD.   O, hear me, Isabella!

Re-enter DUKE

DUKE.   Vouchsafe a word, young sister, but one word.
ISAB.   What is your will?
DUKE.   Might you dispense with your leisure, I would by and by have
    some speech with you: the satisfaction I would require is likewise
    your own benefit.
ISAB.   I have no superfluous leisure; my stay must be stolen out of
    other affairs; but I will attend you awhile.   [*Walks apart.*
DUKE.   Son, I have overheard what hath passed between you and your
    sister. Angelo had never the purpose to corrupt her; only he hath
    made an assay of her virtue to practise his judgement with the dis-
    position of natures:[24] she, having the truth of honour in her, hath
    made him that gracious denial which he is most glad to receive. I
    am confessor to Angelo, and I know this to be true; therefore pre-
    pare yourself to death: do not satisfy your resolution with hopes
    that are fallible:[25] tomorrow you must die; go to your knees, and
    make ready.
CLAUD.   Let me ask my sister pardon. I am so out of love with life, that
    I will sue to be rid of it.
DUKE.   Hold you there: farewell. [*Exit* CLAUDIO.] Provost, a word
    with you!

Re-enter PROVOST

PROV.   What's your will, father?
DUKE.   That now you are come, you will be gone. Leave me awhile
    with the maid: my mind promises with my habit no loss shall
    touch her by my company.
PROV.   In good time.[26]   [*Exit* PROVOST. ISABELLA *comes forward.*
DUKE.   The hand that hath made you fair hath made you good: the
    goodness that is cheap in beauty makes beauty brief in goodness;[27]
    but grace, being the soul of your complexion, shall keep the body

[24]*practise . . . natures*] exercise his judgment in the study of different temperaments.
[25]*do not satisfy . . . fallible*] do not feed your courage with false hopes.
[26]*In good time*] So be it.
[27]*goodness . . . goodness*] When virtue in a beautiful woman is held cheap, her beauty
    does not keep its purity long.

of it ever fair. The assault that Angelo hath made to you, fortune hath conveyed to my understanding; and, but that frailty hath examples for his falling, I should wonder at Angelo. How will you do to content this substitute, and to save your brother?

ISAB.   I am now going to resolve him: I had rather my brother die by the law than my son should be unlawfully born. But, O, how much is the good Duke deceived in Angelo! If ever he return and I can speak to him, I will open my lips in vain, or discover his government.

DUKE.   That shall not be much amiss: yet, as the matter now stands, he will avoid your accusation; he made trial of you only. Therefore fasten your ear on my advisings: to the love I have in doing good a remedy presents itself. I do make myself believe that you may most uprighteously do a poor wronged lady a merited benefit; redeem your brother from the angry law; do no stain to your own gracious person; and much please the absent Duke, if peradventure he shall ever return to have hearing of this business.

ISAB.   Let me hear you speak farther. I have spirit to do any thing that appears not foul in the truth of my spirit.

DUKE.   Virtue is bold, and goodness never fearful. Have you not heard speak of Mariana, the sister of Frederick the great soldier who miscarried at sea?

ISAB.   I have heard of the lady, and good words went with her name.

DUKE.   She should this Angelo have married; was affianced to her by oath, and the nuptial appointed: between which time of the contract and limit of the solemnity,[28] her brother Frederick was wrecked at sea, having in that perished vessel the dowry of his sister. But mark how heavily this befell the poor gentlewoman: there she lost a noble and renowned brother, in his love toward her ever most kind and natural; with him, the portion and sinew of her fortune, her marriage-dowry; with both, her combinate[29] husband, this well-seeming Angelo.

ISAB.   Can this be so? Angelo so leave her?

DUKE.   Left her in her tears, and dried not one of them with his comfort; swallowed his vows whole, pretending in her discoveries of

---

[28]*contract and limit of the solemnity*] the contract of betrothal and the prescribed time within which the wedding ceremony should have taken place.

[29]*combinate*] This word, which is found nowhere else, clearly means "bound," "pledged." It would appear to be formed from "combine," which is occasionally used for "knit together," "pledge."

dishonour: in few, bestowed her on her own lamentation, which she yet wears for his sake; and he, a marble to her tears, is washed with them, but relents not.

ISAB.   What a merit were it in death to take this poor maid from the world! What corruption in this life, that it will let this man live! But how out of this can she avail?

DUKE.   It is a rupture that you may easily heal: and the cure of it not only saves your brother, but keeps you from dishonour in doing it.

ISAB.   Show me how, good father.

DUKE.   This forenamed maid hath yet in her the continuance of her first affection: his unjust unkindness, that in all reason should have quenched her love, hath, like an impediment in the current, made it more violent and unruly. Go you to Angelo; answer his requiring with a plausible obedience; agree with his demands to the point; only refer yourself to this advantage,[30] first, that your stay with him may not be long; that the time may have all shadow and silence in it; and the place answer to convenience. This being granted in course,—and now follows all,—we shall advise this wronged maid to stead up your appointment, go in your place; if the encounter acknowledge itself hereafter, it may compel him to her recompence; and here, by this, is your brother saved, your honour untainted, the poor Mariana advantaged, and the corrupt Deputy scaled.[31] The maid will I frame and make fit for his attempt. If you think well to carry this as you may, the doubleness of the benefit defends the deceit from reproof. What think you of it?

ISAB.   The image of it gives me content already; and I trust it will grow to a most prosperous perfection.

DUKE.   It lies much in your holding up. Haste you speedily to Angelo: if for this night he entreat you to his bed, give him promise of satisfaction. I will presently to Saint Luke's: there, at the moated grange, resides this dejected Mariana. At that place call upon me; and dispatch with Angelo, that it may be quickly.

ISAB.   I thank you for this comfort. Fare you well, good father.

[Exeunt severally.

---

[30]*refer yourself to this advantage*] bear this consideration in mind.

[31]*scaled*] used in a similar sense to that in *Cor.* II, iii, 246, "*scaling* [*i.e.,* weighing] his present bearing with his past." Angelo will be weighed (and found wanting).

SCENE II. *The Street Before the Prison.*

Enter, on one side, DUKE *disguised as before, on the other,* ELBOW, *and Officers with* POMPEY

ELB.   Nay, if there be no remedy for it, but that you will needs buy and sell men and women like beasts, we shall have all the world drink brown and white bastard.[1]

DUKE.   O heavens! what stuff is here?

POM.   'T was never merry world since, of two usuries, the merriest was put down, and the worser allowed by order of law a furred gown[2] to keep him warm; and furred with fox and lamb-skins too, to signify, that craft, being richer than innocency, stands for the facing.

ELB.   Come your way, sir. 'Bless you, good father friar.

DUKE.   And you, good brother father.[3] What offence hath this man made you, sir?

ELB.   Marry, sir, he hath offended the law: and, sir, we take him to be a thief too, sir; for we have found upon him, sir, a strange picklock, which we have sent to the Deputy.

DUKE.   Fie, sirrah! a bawd, a wicked bawd!
The evil that thou causest to be done,
That is thy means to live. Do thou but think
What 't is to cram a maw or clothe a back
From such a filthy vice: say to thyself,
From their abominable and beastly touches
I drink, I eat, array[4] myself, and live.
Canst thou believe thy living is a life,
So stinkingly depending? Go mend, go mend.

POM.   Indeed, it does stink in some sort, sir; but yet, sir, I would prove—

DUKE.   Nay, if the devil have given thee proofs for sin,
Thou wilt prove his. Take him to prison, officer:
Correction and instruction must both work
Ere this rude beast will profit.

ELB.   He must before the Deputy, sir; he has given him warning: the Deputy cannot abide a whoremaster: if he be a whoremonger, and comes before him, he were as good go a mile on his errand.[5]

[1] *bastard*] A pun on the word, which was the name of a sweet Spanish wine.
[2] *a furred gown*] The dress of merchants, whose business often included money-lending. Cf. *Lear*, IV, vi, 163–165: "The *usurer* hangs the cozener . . . Robes and *furr'd gowns* hide all."
[3] *brother father*] a play on Elbow's "father *friar*" (*i.e.*, brother) in the preceding line.
[4] *array*] Theobald's happy emendation for the original *away*.
[5] *he were . . . errand*] he were well out of the way.

DUKE.   That we were all, as some would seem to be,
    From our faults, as faults from seeming, free![6]
ELB.   His neck will come to your waist,—a cord,[7] sir.
POM.   I spy comfort; I cry bail. Here's a gentleman and a friend of
    mine.

Enter LUCIO

LUCIO.   How now, noble Pompey! What, at the wheels of Cæsar? art
    thou led in triumph? What, is there none of Pygmalion's images,
    newly made woman,[8] to be had now, for putting the hand in the
    pocket and extracting it clutched? What reply, ha? What sayest
    thou to this tune, matter and method? Is 't not drowned[9] i' the last
    rain, ha? What sayest thou, Trot?[10] Is the world as it was, man?
    Which is the way? Is it sad, and few words? or how? The trick of
    it?
DUKE.   Still thus, and thus; still worse!
LUCIO.   How doth my dear morsel, thy mistress?
    Procures she still, ha?
POM.   Troth, sir, she hath eaten up all her beef, and she is herself in
    the tub.[11]
LUCIO.   Why, 't is good; it is the right of it; it must be so: ever your
    fresh whore and your powdered bawd: an unshunned[12] conse-
    quence; it must be so. Art going to prison, Pompey?
POM.   Yes, faith, sir.
LUCIO.   Why, 't is not amiss, Pompey. Farewell: go say I sent thee
    thither. For debt, Pompey? or how?
ELB.   For being a bawd, for being a bawd.
LUCIO.   Well, then, imprison him: if imprisonment be the due of a
    bawd, why, 't is his right: bawd is he doubtless, and of antiquity
    too; bawd-born. Farewell, good Pompey. Commend me to the

---

[6]*From our faults, as faults from seeming, free!*] The Duke seems to wish that we were all
as unmistakably true ("free from faults") as downright offenses are innocent of
hypocrisy or the counterfeit of virtue.
[7]*your waist,—a cord*] His neck will be tied like the friar's waist,—with a rope.
[8]*newly made woman*] woman as fresh and untouched as Pygmalion's statue of Galatea,
when it became flesh and blood. Lucio is asking in his frivolous way whether the supply of such unsullied greatness is exhausted, even if one is ready to pay the full price.
[9]*Is 't not drowned, etc.*] A colloquial expression for "are our prospects damped?"
[10]*Trot*] A familiar term of address, usually applied to a bawd or to a decrepit old woman.
Cf. *T. of Shrew,* I, ii, 77–78: "an old *trot* with ne'er a tooth in her head."
[11]*beef . . . tub . . . powdered*] a coarse allusion. Salted or powdered beef was kept in tubs,
and tubs called "sweating tubs," or "powdering tubs," were used in the medicinal
treatment of venereal disease. Cf. *Hen. V,* II, i, 70: "the *powdering [i.e.,* salt]-*tub* of
infamy."
[12]*unshunned*] unshunnable, inevitable.

prison, Pompey: you will turn good husband now, Pompey; you will keep the house.[13]

POM.   I hope, sir, your good worship will be my bail.

LUCIO.   No, indeed, will I not, Pompey; it is not the wear. I will pray, Pompey, to increase your bondage: if you take it not patiently, why, your mettle is the more. Adieu, trusty Pompey. 'Bless you, friar.

DUKE.   And you.

LUCIO.   Does Bridget paint still, Pompey, ha?

ELB.   Come your ways, sir; come.

POM.   You will not bail me, then, sir?

LUCIO.   Then, Pompey, nor now. What news abroad, friar? what news?

ELB.   Come your ways, sir; come.

LUCIO.   Go to kennel, Pompey; go. [*Exeunt* ELBOW, POMPEY *and* Officers.] What news, friar, of the Duke?

DUKE.   I know none. Can you tell me of any?

LUCIO.   Some say he is with the Emperor of Russia; other some, he is in Rome: but where is he, think you?

DUKE.   I know not where; but wheresoever, I wish him well.

LUCIO.   It was a mad fantastical trick of him to steal from the state, and usurp the beggary he was never born to. Lord Angelo dukes it well in his absence; he puts transgression to 't.

DUKE.   He does well in 't.

LUCIO.   A little more lenity to lechery would do no harm in him: something too crabbed that way, friar.

DUKE.   It is too general a vice, and severity must cure it.

LUCIO.   Yes, in good sooth, the vice is of a great kindred; it is well allied: but it is impossible to extirp it quite, friar, till eating and drinking be put down. They say this Angelo was not made by man and woman after this downright way of creation: is it true, think you?

DUKE.   How should he be made, then?

LUCIO.   Some report a sea-maid spawned him; some, that he was begot between two stock-fishes. But it is certain that, when he makes water, his urine is congealed ice; that I know to be true: and he is a motion generative;[14] that's infallible.

DUKE.   You are pleasant, sir, and speak apace.

LUCIO.   Why, what a ruthless thing is this in him, for the rebellion of a codpiece to take away the life of a man! Would the Duke that is

---

[13]*husband . . . house*] an allusion to the etymology of husband from "house," and "band" (*i.e.*, dweller or holder).

[14]*he is a motion generative*] he has the reproductive powers of a puppet or puppet-show.

absent have done this? Ere he would have hanged a man for the
getting a hundred bastards, he would have paid for the nursing a
thousand: he had some feeling of the sport; he knew the service,
and that instructed him to mercy.

DUKE.   I never heard the absent Duke much detected[15] for women;
he was not inclined that way.

LUCIO.   O, sir, you are deceived.

DUKE.   'T is not possible.

LUCIO.   Who, not the Duke? yes, your beggar of fifty; and his use was
to put a ducat in her clack-dish:[16] the Duke had crotchets in him.
He would be drunk too; that let me inform you.

DUKE.   You do him wrong, surely.

LUCIO.   Sir, I was an inward of his. A shy fellow was the Duke: and I
believe I know the cause of his withdrawing.

DUKE.   What, I prithee, might be the cause?

LUCIO.   No, pardon; 't is a secret must be locked within the teeth and
the lips: but this I can let you understand, the greater file of the
subject[17] held the Duke to be wise.

DUKE.   Wise! why, no question but he was.

LUCIO.   A very superficial, ignorant, unweighing fellow.

DUKE.   Either this is envy in you, folly, or mistaking: the very stream
of his life and the business he hath helmed must, upon a warranted need, give him a better proclamation. Let him be but tes-
timonied in his own bringings-forth,[18] and he shall appear to the
envious a scholar, a statesman and a soldier. Therefore you speak
unskilfully; or if your knowledge be more, it is much darkened in
your malice.

LUCIO.   Sir, I know him, and I love him.

DUKE.   Love talks with better knowledge, and knowledge with
dearer[19] love.

LUCIO.   Come, sir, I know what I know.

DUKE.   I can hardly believe that, since you know not what you speak.
But, if ever the Duke return, as our prayers are he may, let me desire you to make your answer before him. If it be honest you have

---

[15]*detected*] "charged," "accused," "arraigned," a common usage. Cf. Hooker, *Eccl.
Polity* (1594): "The gentlewoman . . . *detecteth* herself of a crime."

[16]*clack-dish*] a wooden dish carried by beggars; its movable lid was clacked to attract
notice.

[17]*the greater file of the subject*] the majority of the people.

[18]*the business . . . bringings-forth*] the affairs he has guided (or steered through) must,
on an occasion which warranted (the production of evidence), declare a higher reputation. Let testimony be produced of what he has effected.

[19]*dearer*] Hanmer's emendation of the original *dear*.

spoke, you have courage to maintain it: I am bound to call upon you; and, I pray you, your name?

LUCIO. Sir, my name is Lucio; well known to the Duke.

DUKE. He shall know you better, sir, if I may live to report you.

LUCIO. I fear you not.

DUKE. O, you hope the Duke will return no more; or you imagine me too unhurtful an opposite.[20] But, indeed, I can do you little harm; you'll forswear this again.

LUCIO. I'll be hanged first: thou art deceived in me, friar. But no more of this. Canst thou tell if Claudio die to-morrow or no?

DUKE. Why should he die, sir?

LUCIO. Why? For filling a bottle with a tun-dish. I would the Duke we talk of were returned again: this ungenitured agent[21] will unpeople the province with continency; sparrows must not build in his house-eaves, because they are lecherous. The Duke yet would have dark deeds darkly answered; he would never bring them to light: would he were returned! Marry, this Claudio is condemned for untrussing. Farewell, good friar: I prithee, pray for me. The Duke, I say to thee again, would eat mutton on Fridays.[22] He's not past[23] it yet, and I say to thee, he would mouth with a beggar, though she smelt brown bread and garlic: say that I said so. Farewell. [*Exit.*

DUKE. No might nor greatness in mortality
Can censure 'scape; back-wounding calumny
The whitest virtue strikes. What king so strong
Can tie the gall up in the slanderous tongue?
But who comes here?

Enter ESCALUS, PROVOST, *and* Officers *with* MISTRESS OVERDONE

ESCAL. Go; away with her to prison!

MRS. OV. Good my lord, be good to me; your honour is accounted a merciful man; good my lord.

ESCAL. Double and treble admonition, and still forfeit[24] in the same kind! This would make mercy swear and play the tyrant.

PROV. A bawd of eleven years' continuance, may it please your honour.

MRS. OV. My lord, this is one Lucio's information against me.

---

[20]*too unhurtful an opposite*] too harmless an adversary.

[21]*this ungenitured agent*] this deputy without generative power.

[22]*eat mutton on Fridays*] A pun on mutton in the slang sense of "loose woman." It would be sinful in the Duke, as a pious Catholic, to eat meat on Fridays.

[23]*not past*] Hanmer's sensible emendation of the original *now past.*

[24]*forfeit*] transgress. In early English this is the usual meaning of the word.

Mistress Kate Keepdown was with child by him in the Duke's
time; he promised her marriage: his child is a year and a quarter
old, come Philip and Jacob:[25] I have kept it myself; and see how
he goes about to abuse me!

ESCAL.   That fellow is a fellow of much license: let him be called before us. Away with her to prison! Go to; no more words.

                             [*Exeunt* Officers *with* MISTRESS OV.]
Provost, my brother Angelo will not be altered; Claudio must die
to-morrow: let him be furnished with divines, and have all chari-
table preparation. If my brother wrought by my pity, it should not
be so with him.

PROV.   So please you, this friar hath been with him, and advised him
for the entertainment of death.

ESCAL.   Good even, good father.

DUKE.   Bliss and goodness on you!

ESCAL.   Of whence are you?

DUKE.   Not of this country, though my chance is now
        To use it for my time: I am a brother
        Of gracious order, late come from the See[26]
        In special business from his Holiness.

ESCAL.   What news abroad i' the world?

DUKE.   None, but that there is so great a fever on goodness, that the
        dissolution of it must cure it: novelty is only in request; and it as
        dangerous to be aged in any kind of course, as it is virtuous to be
        constant in any undertaking. There is scarce truth enough alive to
        make societies secure; but security enough to make fellowships ac-
        curst:[27]—much upon this riddle runs the wisdom of the world.
        This news is old enough, yet it is every day's news. I pray you, sir,
        of what disposition was the Duke?

ESCAL.   One that, above all other strifes, contended especially to know
        himself.

DUKE.   What pleasure was he given to?

ESCAL.   Rather rejoicing to see another merry, than merry at any thing
        which professed to make him rejoice: a gentleman of all temper-
        ance. But leave we him to his events,[28] with a prayer they
        may prove prosperous; and let me desire to know how you find

---

[25]*come Philip and Jacob*] a reference to the first of May, the festival of the apostles SS.
   Philip and James (Lat. Jacobus).

[26]*the See*] the See of Rome.

[27]*but security . . . accurst*] Here "security" means "the act of standing surety" (for an em-
   barrassed acquaintance, with the prospect of ruin to one's own estate). Social relations
   (*i.e.*, fellowships) are cursed by the commonness of the practice. Cf. Proverbs xi, 15:
   "He that is surety for a stranger shall smart for it; and he that hateth suretiship is sure."

[28]*events*] fortunes.

Claudio prepared. I am made to understand that you have lent him visitation.

DUKE. He professes to have received no sinister measure from his judge, but most willingly humbles himself to the determination of justice: yet had he framed to himself, by the instruction of his frailty, many deceiving promises of life; which I, by my good leisure, have discredited to him, and now is he resolved to die.

ESCAL. You have paid the heavens your function,[29] and the prisoner the very debt of your calling. I have laboured for the poor gentleman to the extremest shore of my modesty: but my brother justice have I found so severe, that he hath forced me to tell him he is indeed Justice.[30]

DUKE. If his own life answer the straitness of his proceeding, it shall become him well; wherein if he chance to fail, he hath sentenced himself.

ESCAL. I am going to visit the prisoner. Fare you well.

DUKE. Peace be with you!   [*Exeunt* ESCALUS *and* PROVOST.

He who the sword of heaven will bear
Should be as holy as severe;
Pattern in himself to know,
Grace to stand, and virtue go;[31]
More nor less to others paying
Than by self-offenses weighing.
Shame to him whose cruel striking
Kills for faults of his own liking!
Twice treble shame on Angelo,
To weed my vice[32] and let his grow!
O, what may man within him hide,
Though angel on the outward side!
How may likeness made in crimes,
Making practice on the times,
To draw with idle spiders' strings
Most ponderous and substantial things![33]
Craft against vice I must apply:

---

[29]*have . . . your function*] discharged your duty to Heaven.

[30]*he is indeed Justice*] An allusion to the maxim "Summum jus, summa injuria."

[31]*Grace . . . virtue go*] Grace whereon to stand secure (against temptation), and virtue wherewith to walk.

[32]*To weed my vice*] To uproot another's vice.

[33]*How may likeness . . . substantial things*] "Likeness" is probably identical with "seeming" (*i.e.*, hypocrisy, the counterfeit of virtue). The general meaning is that hypocrisy, the product of crimes, which plot against or hoodwink the age, is capable, by means of frauds, flimsy as spiders' threads, of capturing weighty and substantial objects like riches and power.

With Angelo to-night shall lie
His old betrothed but despised;
So disguise shall, by the disguised,
Pay with falsehood false exacting,
And perform an old contracting.[34]   [*Exit.*

---

[34]*So disguise shall . . . contracting*] Thus the Folios. The words are difficult to interpret.
The meaning seems to be that the disguise which Mariana is assuming will, by the
agency of the vicious Angelo, who wears the *false guise* of sanctity, satisfy deceptively
his base demand, and fulfill an old standing contract.

ACT IV.

SCENE I. *The Moated Grange at St. Luke's.*

Enter MARIANA *and a* Boy.
Boy *sings*

> Take, o, take those lips way,
> That so sweetly were forsworn;
> And those eyes, the break of day,
> Lights that do mislead the morn:
> But my kisses bring again, bring again;
> Seals of love, but seal'd in vain, seal'd in vain.[1,2]

MARI.   Break off thy song, and haste thee quick away:
    Here comes a man of comfort, whose advise
    Hath often still'd my brawling discontent.   [*Exit* Boy.

Enter DUKE *disguised as before*

    I cry you mercy, sir; and well could wish
    You had not found me here so musical:
    Let me excuse me, and believe me so,
    My mirth it much displeased, but pleased my woe.[3]
DUKE.   'T is good; though music oft hath such a charm
    To make bad good, and good provoke to harm.
    I pray you, tell me, hath any body inquired for me here to-day?
    much upon this time have I promised here to meet.[4]

---

[1]This stanza is repeated with the addition of a second stanza by Fletcher in the latter's
Bloody Brother, or Rollo Duke of Normandy, in Act V, Sc. 2. The two stanzas reappear
together in Shakespeare's *Poems,* 1640. Shakespeare's exclusive responsibility for the
first stanza need not be questioned.
[2]*Seals of love . . . in vain*] Cf. *Sonnet* cxlii, 5–7, "those lips of thine . . . *seal'd false bonds
of love* as oft of mine."
[3]*My mirth . . . woe*] The music was out of tune with any disposition to merriment on
my part, but it assuaged my sorrow.
[4]*meet*] often used intransitively by Shakespeare. Cf. *As You Like It,* V, ii, 111–112, "as
you love Phoebe, *meet*: and as I love no woman, I'll *meet.*"

MARI.   You have not been inquired after: I have sat here all day.

Enter ISABELLA

DUKE.   I do constantly believe you. The time is come even now. I
     shall crave your forbearance a little: may be I will call upon you
     anon, for some advantage to yourself.

MARI.   I am always bound to you.   [*Exit.*

DUKE.   Very well met, and well come.
     What is the news from this good Deputy?

ISAB.   He hath a garden circummured with brick,
     Whose western side is with a vineyard back'd;
     And to that vineyard is a planched[5] gate,
     That makes his opening[6] with this bigger key:
     This other doth command a little door
     Which from the vineyard to the garden leads;
     There have I made my promise
     Upon the heavy middle of the night
     To call upon him.[7]

DUKE.   But shall you on your knowledge find this way?

ISAB.   I have ta'en a due and wary note upon 't:
     With whispering and most guilty diligence,
     In action all of precept,[8] he did show me
     The way twice o'er.

DUKE.   Are there no other tokens
     Between you 'greed concerning her observance?[9]

ISAB.   No, none, but only a repair i' the dark;
     And that I have possess'd him my most stay
     Can be but brief; for I have made him know
     I have a servant comes with me along,
     That stays upon me, whose persuasion is
     I come about my brother.

DUKE.   'T is well borne up.
     I have not yet made known to Mariana
     A word of this. What, ho! within! come forth!

Re-enter MARIANA

     I pray you, be acquainted with this maid;
     She comes to do you good.

[5]*planched*] made of planks.
[6]*his opening*] its opening, *i.e.*, the opening of the gate.
[7]*There have . . . upon him*] In the Folios these three lines are printed as two, the second
  line beginning at "heavy." Possibly Isabella suddenly lapses into prose.
[8]*In action . . . precept*] Giving direction only by action, gesture.
[9]*her observance*] her keeping the appointment.

ISAB.　　　　　　　　　　　I do desire the like.
DUKE.　　Do you persuade yourself that I respect you?
MARI.　　Good friar, I know you do, and have found it.
DUKE.　　Take, then, this your companion by the hand,
　　　Who hath a story ready for your ear.
　　　I shall attend your leisure: but make haste;
　　　The vaporous night approaches.
MARI.　　Will 't please you walk aside?

　　　　　　　　　　　　　　　[*Exeunt* MARIANA *and* ISABELLA.

DUKE.　　O place and greatness, millions of false eyes[10]
　　　Are stuck upon thee! volumes of report
　　　Run with these false and most contrarious quests
　　　Upon thy doings! thousand escapes of wit[11]
　　　Make thee the father of their idle dreams,
　　　And rack thee in their fancies!

Re-enter MARIANA *and* ISABELLA

　　　　　　　　　　　　　Welcome, how agreed?
ISAB.　　She'll take the enterprise upon her, father,
　　　If you advise it.
DUKE.　　　　　　　It is not my consent,
　　　But my entreaty too.
ISAB.　　　　　　　　Little have you to say
　　　When you depart from him, but, soft and low,
　　　"Remember now my brother."
MARI.　　　　　　　　　　Fear me not.
DUKE.　　Nor, gentle daughter, fear you not at all.
　　　He is your husband on a pre-contract:
　　　To bring you thus together, 't is no sin,
　　　Sith that the justice of your title to him
　　　Doth flourish the deceit.[12] Come, let us go:
　　　Our corn's to reap, for yet our tithe's to sow.[13]

　　　　　　　　　　　　　　　　　　　　[*Exeunt.*

---

[10]*false eyes*] insidious, treacherous eyes.
[11]*Run . . . escapes of wit*] Overflow with lying and self-contradictory prying inquiries into thy doings! thousand sportive and scurrilous sallies of wit, etc.
[12]*flourish the deceit*] make the deceit fair or reputable. Cf. *Tw. Night*, III, iv, 354: "empty trunks, *o'erflourish'd* [*i.e.*, glossed or varnished over] by the devil."
[13]*Our corn . . . sow*] Dr. Johnson conjectured this expression to be proverbial, and regarded "tithe" as standing for "harvest." It is probably to be used for "grain." Theobald and others recommend the substitution for *tithe*, of *tilth, i.e.*, land ready for sowing. But "tithe" in the sense of "grain" makes the line intelligible.

SCENE II. *A Room in the Prison.*

Enter PROVOST *and* POMPEY

PROV.   Come hither, sirrah. Can you cut off a man's head?

POM.   If the man be a bachelor, sir, I can; but if he be a married man,
he's his wife's head, and I can never cut off a woman's head.

PROV.   Come, sir, leave me your snatches, and yield me a direct answer. To-morrow morning are to die Claudio and Barnardine.
Here is in our prison a common executioner, who in his office
lacks a helper: if you will take it on you to assist him, it shall redeem you from your gyves; if not, you shall have your full time of
imprisonment, and your deliverance with an unpitied whipping,
for you have been a notorious bawd.

POM.   Sir, I have been an unlawful bawd time out of mind; but yet I
will be content to be a lawful hangman. I would be glad to receive
some instruction from my fellow partner.

PROV.   What, ho! Abhorson! Where's Abhorson, there?

Enter ABHORSON

ABHOR. Do you call, sir?

PROV.   Sirrah, here's a fellow will help you to-morrow in your execution. If you think it meet, compound with him by the year, and let
him abide here with you; if not, use him for the present, and dismiss him. He cannot plead his estimation with you; he hath been
a bawd.

ABHOR. A bawd, sir? fie upon him! he will discredit our mystery.

PROV.   Go to, sir; you weigh equally; a feather will turn the scale.

[*Exit.*

POM.   Pray, sir, by your good favour,—for surely, sir, a good favour you
have, but that you have a hanging look,—do you call, sir, your occupation a mystery?[1]

ABHOR. Ay, sir; a mystery.

POM.   Painting, sir, I have heard say, is a mystery; and your whores, sir,
being members of my occupation, using painting, do prove my occupation a mystery: but what mystery there should be in hanging,
if I should be hanged, I cannot imagine.

ABHOR. Sir, it is a mystery.

POM.   Proof?

ABHOR. Every true man's apparel fits your thief: if it be too little for

---

[1]*mystery*] "Mystery," in the sense of calling or trade (from the Latin *ministerium*), has
no etymological connection with "mystery" in the sense of a secret rite (from the
Greek μυστήριον). The two words are here punningly confused.

your thief, your true man thinks it big enough; if it be too big for
your thief, your thief thinks it little enough: so every true man's apparel fits your thief.[2]

Re-enter PROVOST

PROV.   Are you agreed?
POM.   Sir, I will serve him; for I do find your hangman is a more pen-
itent trade than your bawd; he doth oftener ask forgiveness.[3]
PROV.   You, sirrah, provide your block and your axe to-morrow four
o'clock.
ABHOR.   Come on, bawd; I will instruct thee in my trade; follow.
POM.   I do desire to learn, sir: and I hope, if you have occasion to use
me for your own turn, you shall find me yare; for, truly, sir, for
your kindness I owe you a good turn.[4]
PROV.   Call hither Barnardine and Claudio:

[*Exeunt* POMPEY *and* ABHORSON.

The one has my pity; not a jot the other,
Being a murderer, though he were my brother.

Enter CLAUDIO

Look, here's the warrant, Claudio, for thy death:
'T is now dead midnight, and by eight to-morrow
Thou must be made immortal. Where's Barnardine?
CLAUD.   As fast lock'd up in sleep as guiltless labour
When it lies starkly in the traveller's bones:
He will not wake.
PROV.   Who can do good on him?
Well, go, prepare yourself. [*Knocking within.*] But, hark, what
noise?—
Heaven give your spirits comfort! [*Exit* CLAUDIO.] By and by.—
I hope it is some pardon or reprieve
For the most gentle Claudio.

Enter DUKE *disguised as before*

Welcome, father.

[2]*if it be too little . . . fits your thief*] The Folios assign this part of the speech to Pompey,
and the poor choplogic which seeks to identify the honest man with the thief seems to
be in his vein. But Capell and most succeeding editors transferred these far-fetched
quibbles to the cynical hangman on the reasonable ground that they suggest professional knowledge, which Pompey would be unlikely to claim.
[3]*ask forgiveness*] Cf. *As You Like It*, III, v, 3–6, "The common *executioner . . . first begs
pardon*" (of his victim).
[4]*a good turn*] a turn off the ladder, on which the convict mounts the gallows; a slang
term for a hanging.

DUKE.   The best and wholesomest spirits of the night
    Envelop you, good Provost! Who call'd here of late?
PROV.   None, since the curfew rung.
DUKE.   Not Isabel?
PROV.   No.
DUKE.   They[5] will, then, ere 't be long.
PROV.   What comfort is for Claudio?
DUKE.   There's some in hope.
PROV.   It is a bitter deputy.
DUKE.   Not so, not so; his life is parallel'd
    Even with the stroke and line of his great justice:[6]
    He doth with holy abstinence subdue
    That in himself which he spurs on his power
    To qualify in others: were he meal'd[7] with that
    Which he corrects, then were he tyrannous;
    But this being so, he's just.   [*Knocking within.*
                   Now are they come.
                             [*Exit* PROVOST.
    This is a gentle provost: seldom when
    The steeled gaoler is the friend of men.   [*Knocking within.*
    How now! what noise? That spirit's possess'd with haste
    That wounds the unsisting[8] postern with these strokes.

Re-enter PROVOST

PROV.   There he must stay until the officer
    Arise to let him in: he is call'd up.
DUKE.   Have you no countermand for Claudio yet,
    But he must die to-morrow?
PROV.   None, sir, none.
DUKE.   As near the dawning, provost, as it is,
    You shall hear more ere morning.
PROV.   Happily
    You something know; yet I believe there comes
    No countermand; no such example have we:
    Besides, upon the very siege[9] of justice

---

[5]*They*] The Duke expects Mariana as well as Isabella.
[6]*his life . . . justice*] his life runs parallel or square with the mark and character of his high conception of justice.
[7]*meal'd*] stained, defiled. Cf. *Macb.*, IV, i, 123: "blood-*bolter'd* Banquo."
[8]*unsisting*] Thus the first three Folios. The Fourth Folio substitutes *insisting*, and Rowe conjectured *unresisting*. "Unsisting" is unknown elsewhere. The meaning would seem to be that the postern gate offers comparatively small resistance.
[9]*siege*] seat. Cf. Spenser's *Faerie Queene*, II, iv, 44, line 5, "A stately *siege* [*i.e.*, seat, throne] of sovereign majesty."

Lord Angelo hath to the public ear
Profess'd the contrary.

Enter a Messenger

This is his lordship's man.[10]

DUKE. And here comes Claudio's pardon.
MES. [*Giving a paper*] My lord hath sent you this note; and by me
this further charge, that you swerve not from the smallest article of
it, neither in time, matter, or other circumstance. Good morrow;
for, as I take it, it is almost day.
PROV. I shall obey him. [*Exit* MESSENGER.
DUKE. [*Aside*] This is his pardon, purchased by such sin
For which the pardoner himself is in.
Hence hath offence his quick celerity,
When it is borne in high authority:
When vice makes mercy, mercy's so extended,
That for the fault's love is the offender friended.
Now, sir, what news?
PROV. I told you. Lord Angelo, belike thinking me remiss in mine of-
fice, awakens me with this unwonted putting-on;[11] methinks
strangely, for he hath not used it before.
DUKE. Pray you, let's hear.
PROV. [*Reads*]

Whatsoever you may hear to the contrary, let Claudio be executed by
four of the clock; and in the afternoon Barnardine: for my better satisfaction, let me have Claudio's head sent me by five. Let this be duly per-
formed; with a thought that more depends on it than we must yet deliver. Thus fail not to do your office, as you will answer it at your peril.

What say you to this, sir?
DUKE. What is that Barnardine who is to be executed in the afternoon?
PROV. A Bohemian born, but here nursed up and bred; one that is a
prisoner nine years old.
DUKE. How came it that the absent Duke had not either delivered
him to his liberty or executed him? I have heard it was ever his
manner to do so.
PROV. His friends still wrought reprieves for him: and, indeed, his
fact, till now in the government of Lord Angelo, came not to an
undoubtful proof.

[10]*This is his lordship's man*] In the Folios this sentence is given to the Duke, and the
following one to the provost. The change in the text, though generally adopted, is not
essential.
[11]*putting-on*] spur, incitement. The verb "put on" is often used thus.

DUKE.   It is now apparent?

PROV.   Most manifest, and not denied by himself.

DUKE.   Hath he borne himself penitently in prison? how seems he to be touched?

PROV.   A man that apprehends death no more dreadfully but as a drunken sleep; careless, reckless, and fearless of what's past, present, or to come; insensible of mortality, and desperately mortal.[12]

DUKE.   He wants advice.

PROV.   He will hear none: he hath evermore had the liberty of the prison; give him leave to escape hence, he would not: drunk many times a day, if not many days entirely drunk. We have very oft awaked him, as if to carry him to execution, and showed him a seeming warrant for it: it hath not moved him at all.

DUKE.   More of him anon. There is written in your brow, provost, honesty and constancy: if I read it not truly, my ancient skill beguiles me; but, in the boldness of my cunning, I will lay myself in hazard.[13] Claudio, whom here you have warrant to execute, is no greater forfeit to the law than Angelo who hath sentenced him. To make you understand this in a manifest effect, I crave but four days' respite; for the which you are to do me both a present and a dangerous courtesy.

PROV.   Pray, sir, in what?

DUKE.   In the delaying death.

PROV.   Alack, how may I do it, having the hour limited, and an express command, under penalty, to deliver his head in the view of Angelo? I may make my case as Claudio's, to cross this in the smallest.

DUKE.   By the vow of mine order I warrant you, if my instructions may be your guide. Let this Barnardine be this morning executed, and his head borne to Angelo.

PROV.   Angelo hath seen them both, and will discover the favour.

DUKE.   O, death's a great disguiser; and you may add to it. Shave the head, and tie the beard; and say it was the desire of the penitent to be so bared[14] before his death: you know the course is common. If any thing fall to you upon this, more than thanks and good fortune, by the Saint whom I profess, I will plead against it with my life.

PROV.   Pardon me, good father; it is against my oath.

DUKE.   Were you sworn to the Duke, or to the Deputy?

---

[12]*desperately mortal*] either hopelessly involved in mortal sin, or likely to die hopeless and unrepentant.

[13]*in the boldness . . . hazard*] confident in my sagacity, I will run the risk.

[14]*bared*] shaved. Cf. *All's Well*, IV, i, 46: "the *baring* of my beard."

PROV. To him, and to his substitutes.

DUKE. You will think you have made no offence, if the Duke avouch the justice of your dealing?

PROV. But what likelihood is in that?

DUKE. Not a resemblance, but a certainty. Yet since I see you fearful, that neither my coat, integrity, nor persuasion can with ease attempt[15] you, I will go further than I meant, to pluck all fears out of you. Look you, sir, here is the hand and seal of the Duke: you know the character, I doubt not; and the signet is not strange to you.

PROV. I know them both.

DUKE. The contents of this is the return of the Duke: you shall anon over-read it at your pleasure; where you shall find, within these two days he will be here. This is a thing that Angelo knows not; for he this very day receives letters of strange tenour; perchance of the Duke's death; perchance entering into some monastery; but, by chance, nothing of what is writ. Look, the unfolding star[16] calls up the shepherd. Put not yourself into amazement how these things should be: all difficulties are but easy when they are known. Call your executioner, and off with Barnardine's head: I will give him a present shrift and advise him for a better place. Yet you are amazed; but this shall absolutely resolve you. Come away; it is almost clear dawn.   [*Exeunt.*

SCENE III. *Another Room in the Same.*

Enter POMPEY

POM. I am as well acquainted here as I was in our house of profession:[1] one would think it were Mistress Overdone's own house, for here be many of her old customers. First, here's young Master Rash; he's in for a commodity of brown paper and old ginger,[2] nine-score and seventeen pounds; of which he made five marks, ready money: marry, then ginger was not much in request, for the old women were all dead.[3] Then is there here one Master Caper,

---

[15]*attempt*] tempt. Cf. *Merch. of Ven.*, IV, i, 416, "of force I must *attempt* you further."

[16]*the unfolding star*] the morning star. Cf. Milton's *Comus*, 94–95 [of the evening star]: "The star that bids the *shepherd fold*, Now the top of heaven doth hold."

[1]*house of profession*] a house professedly applied to immoral uses.

[2]*brown paper and old ginger*] worthless articles foisted by money-lenders as things of value on foolish borrowers.

[3]*ginger . . . dead*] See *Merch. of Ven.*, III, i, 9: "As lying a gossip in that as ever knapped ginger."

at the suit of Master Three-pile the mercer, for some four suits of peach-coloured satin, which now peaches him a beggar.[4] Then have we here young Dizy, and young Master Deep-vow, and Master Copper-spur, and Master Starve-lackey the rapier and dagger man,[5] and young Drop-heir that killed lusty Pudding, and Master Forthlight the tilter, and brave Master Shooty[6] the great traveller, and wild Half-can that stabbed Pots, and, I think, forty more; all great doers in our trade, and are now "for the Lord's sake."[7]

Enter ABHORSON

ABHOR.   Sirrah, bring Barnardine hither.

POM.   Master Barnardine! you must rise and be hanged, Master Barnardine!

ABHOR.   What, ho, Barnardine!

BAR.   [*Within*] A pox o' your throats! Who makes that noise there? What are you?

POM.   Your friends, sir; the hangman. You must be so good, sir, to rise and be put to death.

BAR.   [*Within*] Away, you rogue, away! I am sleepy.

ABHOR.   Tell him he must awake, and that quickly too.

POM.   Pray, Master Barnardine, awake till you are executed, and sleep afterwards.

ABHOR.   Go in to him, and fetch him out.

POM.   He is coming, sir, he is coming; I hear his straw rustle.

ABHOR.   Is the axe upon the block, sirrah?

POM.   Very ready, sir.

Enter BARNARDINE

BAR.   How now, Abhorson? what's the news with you?

ABHOR.   Truly, sir, I would desire you to clap into your prayers; for, look you, the warrant's come.

BAR.   You rogue, I have been drinking all night; I am not fitted for 't.

POM.   O, the better, sir; for he that drinks all night, and is hanged betimes in the morning, may sleep the sounder all the next day.

---

[4]*peaches him a beggar*] supplies the evidence that he is a beggar.

[5]*rapier and dagger man*] the duelist who usually fought with both weapons.

[6]*Shooty*] Thus the Second and later Folios. The First Folio reads *Shootie, i.e.,* shoe-tie. The reasonable suggestion that the reference is to Tom Coryate, who made his reputation by walking to Venice and back in the same pair of shoes in 1608, can only be adopted if we assume that the words were interpolated after the first production of the play in 1604.

[7]*"for the Lord's sake"*] This was the common cry with which prisoners begged from behind the prison bars of passersby.

ABHOR. Look you, sir; here comes your ghostly father: do we jest now, think you?

Enter DUKE *disguised as before*

DUKE. Sir, induced by my charity, and hearing how hastily you are to depart, I am come to advise you, comfort you and pray with you.

BAR. Friar, not I: I have been drinking hard all night, and I will have more time to prepare me, or they shall beat out my brains with billets: I will not consent to die this day, that's certain.

DUKE. O, sir, you must: and therefore I beseech you
Look forward on the journey you shall go.

BAR. I swear I will not die to-day for any man's persuasion.

DUKE. But hear you.

BAR. Not a word: if you have any thing to say to me, come to my ward; for thence will not I to-day. [*Exit.*

DUKE. Unfit to live or die: O gravel heart!
After him, fellows; bring him to the block.
[*Exeunt* ABHORSON *and* POMPEY.

Enter PROVOST

PROV. Now, sir, how do you find the prisoner?

DUKE. A creature unprepared, unmeet for death;
And to transport him in the mind he is
Were damnable.

PROV. Here in the prison, father,
There died this morning of a cruel fever
One Ragozine, a most notorious pirate,
A man of Claudio's years; his beard and head
Just of his colour. What if we do omit
This reprobate till he were well inclined;
And satisfy the Deputy with the visage
Of Ragozine, more like to Claudio?

DUKE. O, 't is an accident that heaven provides!
Dispatch it presently; the hour draws on
Prefix'd by Angelo: see this be done,
And sent according to command; whiles I
Persuade this rude wretch willingly to die.

PROV. This shall be done, good father, presently.
But Barnardine must die this afternoon:
And how shall we continue[8] Claudio,
To save me from the danger that might come
If he were known alive?

8*continue*] keep.

DUKE.   Let this be done.
   Put them in secret holds, both Barnardine and Claudio:
   Ere twice the sun hath made his journal greeting
   To the under generation,[9] you shall find
   Your safety manifested.
PROV.   I am your free dependant.
DUKE.   Quick, dispatch, and send the head to Angelo.

                                   [*Exit* PROVOST.

   Now will I write letters to Angelo,—
   The provost, he shall bear them,—whose contents
   Shall witness to him I am near at home,
   And that, by great injunctions, I am bound
   To enter publicly: him I'll desire
   To meet me at the consecrated fount,
   A league below the city; and from thence,
   By cold gradation and well-balanced form,
   We shall proceed with Angelo.

Re-enter PROVOST

PROV.   Here is the head; I'll carry it myself.
DUKE.   Convenient is it. Make a swift return;
   For I would commune with you of such things
   That want no ear but yours.
PROV.   I'll make all speed.   [*Exit.*
ISAB.   [*Within*] Peace, ho, be here!
DUKE.   The tongue of Isabel. She's come to know
   If yet her brother's pardon be come hither:
   But I will keep her ignorant of her good,
   To make her heavenly comforts of despair,
   When it is least expected.[10]

Enter ISABELLA

ISAB.   Ho, by your leave!
DUKE.   Good morning to you, fair and gracious daughter.
ISAB.   The better, given me by so holy a man.
   Hath yet the Deputy sent my brother's pardon?

---

[9]*his journal greeting . . . generation*] The Folios here read *yond* (for *the under*) *genera-tion*, which Rowe extended to *yonder generation.* Hanmer sensibly proposed *the under generation*, understanding that the words referred to the sun's daily greeting of the Antipodes. Cf. *Rich. II*, III, ii, 37–38: "the searching eye of heaven is hid, Behind the globe, that lights the *lower world.*"

[10]*To . . . expected*] To cause her despair to give place to happiness when she least looked for it.

DUKE.   He hath released him, Isabel, from the world:
　　　His head is off, and sent to Angelo.
ISAB.   Nay, but it is not so.
DUKE.   It is no other: show your wisdom, daughter,
　　　In your close patience.
ISAB.   O, I will to him and pluck out his eyes!
DUKE.   You shall not be admitted to his sight.
ISAB.   Unhappy Claudio! wretched Isabel!
　　　Injurious world! most damned Angelo!
DUKE.   This nor hurts him nor profits you a jot;
　　　Forbear it therefore; give your cause to heaven.
　　　Mark what I say, which you shall find
　　　By every syllable a faithful verity:
　　　The Duke comes home to-morrow;—nay, dry your eyes;
　　　One of our covent,[11] and his confessor,
　　　Gives me this instance:[12] already he hath carried
　　　Notice to Escalus and Angelo;
　　　Who do prepare to meet him at the gates,
　　　There to give up their power. If you can, pace your wisdom
　　　In that good path that I would wish it go;
　　　And you shall have your bosom[13] on this wretch,
　　　Grace of the Duke, revenges to your heart,
　　　And general honour.
ISAB.　　　　　　　　　　I am directed by you.
DUKE.   This letter, then, to Friar Peter give;
　　　'T is that he sent me of the Duke's return:
　　　Say, by this token, I desire his company
　　　At Mariana's house to-night. Her cause and yours
　　　I'll perfect him withal; and he shall bring you
　　　Before the Duke; and to the head of Angelo
　　　Accuse him home and home. For my poor self,
　　　I am combined[14] by a sacred vow,
　　　And shall be absent. Wend you with this letter:
　　　Command these fretting waters from your eyes
　　　With a light heart; trust not my holy order,
　　　If I pervert your course.—Who's here?

Enter LUCIO

LUCIO.   Good even. Friar, where's the provost?

---

[11]*covent*] Thus the Folios: a variant of "convent," as in *Covent* Garden.
[12]*instance*] assurance, intimation.
[13]*bosom*] heart's desire.
[14]*combined*] bound, pledged.

DUKE.   Not within, sir.

LUCIO.   O pretty Isabella, I am pale at mine heart to see thine eyes so red: thou must be patient. I am fain to dine and sup with water and bran; I dare not for my head fill my belly; one fruitful meal would set me to 't. But they say the Duke will be here to-morrow. By my troth, Isabel, I loved thy brother: if the old fantastical Duke of dark corners had been at home, he had lived.   [*Exit* ISABELLA.

DUKE.   Sir, the Duke is marvellous little beholding to your reports; but the best is, he lives not in them.

LUCIO.   Friar, thou knowest not the Duke so well as I do: he's a better woodman[15] than thou takest him for.

DUKE.   Well, you'll answer this one day. Fare ye well.

LUCIO.   Nay, tarry; I'll go along with thee: I can tell thee pretty tales of the Duke.

DUKE.   You have told me too many of him already, sir, if they be true; if not true, none were enough.

LUCIO.   I was once before him for getting a wench with child.

DUKE.   Did you such a thing?

LUCIO.   Yes, marry, did I: but I was fain to forswear it; they would else have married me to the rotten medlar.

DUKE.   Sir, your company is fairer than honest. Rest you well.

LUCIO.   By my troth, I'll go with thee to the lane's end: if bawdy talk offend you, we'll have very little of it. Nay, friar, I am a kind of burr; I shall stick.   [*Exeunt.*

SCENE IV. *A Room in Angelo's House.*

Enter ANGELO *and* ESCALUS

ESCAL.   Every letter he hath writ hath disvouched other.

ANG.   In most uneven and distracted manner. His actions show much like to madness: pray heaven his wisdom be not tainted! And why meet him at the gates, and redeliver[1] our authorities there?

ESCAL.   I guess not.

ANG.   And why should we proclaim it in an hour before his entering, that if any crave redress of injustice, they should exhibit their petitions in the street?

[15]*woodman*] Used colloquially of a hunter after female game, or women. Cf. *M. Wives*, V, v, 25: "Am I *a woodman*, ha?" Also see Beaumont and Fletcher's *The Chances*, I, viii, "I see you are *a woodman* and can choose your deer tho' it be i' the dark."

[1]*redeliver*] This is Capell's emendation of the *reliver* of the First Folio, and *deliver* of the Second and later Folios. Shakespeare possibly had in mind the French verb "relivrer," which Cotgrave interprets as "redeliver."

ESCAL.   He shows his reason for that: to have a dispatch of complaints,
   and to deliver us from devices hereafter, which shall then have no
   power to stand against us.
ANG.   Well, I beseech you, let it be proclaimed betimes i' the morn;
   I'll call you at your house: give notice to such men of sort and suit[2]
   as are to meet him.
ESCAL.   I shall, sir. Fare you well.
ANG.   Good night.   [*Exit* ESCALUS.
   This deed unshapes me quite, makes me unpregnant,
   And dull to all proceedings. A deflower'd maid!
   And by an eminent body that enforced
   The law against it! But that her tender shame
   Will not proclaim against her maiden loss,
   How might she tongue me! Yet reason dares her no;[3]
   For my authority bears of a credent[4] bulk,
   That no particular scandal once can touch
   But it confounds the breather. He should have lived,
   Save that this riotous youth, with dangerous sense,
   Might in the times to come have ta'en revenge,
   By so receiving a dishonour'd life
   With ransom of such shame. Would yet he had lived!
   Alack, when once our grace we have forgot,
   Nothing goes right: we would, and we would not.   [*Exit.*

SCENE V. *Fields Without the Town.*

Enter DUKE *in his own habit, and* FRIAR PETER

DUKE.   These letters at fit time deliver me: [*Giving letters.*
   The provost knows our purpose and our plot.
   The matter being afoot, keep your instruction,
   And hold you ever to our special drift;
   Though sometimes you do blench[1] from this to that,
   As cause doth minister. Go call at Flavius' house,
   And tell him where I stay: give the like notice
   To Valentius, Rowland, and to Crassus,

---

[2]*sort and suit*] men of rank, owing suit and service to their feudal lord.
[3]*dares her no*] Thus the Folios. The language, though crabbed, is quite plain. Reason
 warns her not to employ her tongue.
[4]*bears of a credent*] supports such great weight of credit.

---

[1]*blench*] "Blench," which commonly means "start in fright," here has the weaker sig-
 nificance of "diverge," "move away."

And bid them bring the trumpets to the gate;
But send me Flavius first.
FRI. P.   It shall be speeded well.   [*Exit.*

Enter VARRIUS

DUKE.   I thank thee, Varrius; thou hast made good haste:
Come, we will walk. There's other of our friends
Will greet us here anon, my gentle Varrius.   [*Exeunt.*

SCENE VI. *Street Near the City Gate.*

Enter ISABELLA *and* MARIANA

ISAB.   To speak so indirectly I am loath:
I would say the truth; but to accuse him so,
That is your part: yet I am advised to do it;
He says, to veil full[1] purpose.
MARI.   Be ruled by him.
ISAB.   Besides, he tells me that, if peradventure
He speak against me on the adverse side,
I should not think it strange; for 't is a physic
That's bitter to sweet end.
MARI.   I would Friar Peter—
ISAB.   O, peace! the friar is come.

Enter FRIAR PETER

FRI. P.   Come, I have found you out a stand most fit,
Where you may have such vantage on the Duke,
He shall not pass you. Twice have the trumpets sounded;
The generous and gravest citizens
Have hent the gates,[2] and very near upon
The Duke is entering: therefore, hence, away!   [*Exeunt.*

---

[1]*to veil full*] Malone's emendation of *to vaile full* of the Folios. Theobald adopted *t' availful,* which he interpreted "to profitable purpose."
[2]*The generous . . . gates*] The high-born and most influential citizens have reached the gates.

ACT V.

SCENE I. *The City Gate.*

MARIANA *veiled,* ISABELLA, *and* FRIAR PETER, *at their stand. Enter*
DUKE, VARRIUS, Lords, ANGELO, ESCALUS, LUCIO, PROVOST,
Officers, *and* Citizens, *at several doors*

DUKE. My very worthy cousin, fairly met!
   Our old and faithful friend, we are glad to see you.

ANG. }
ESCAL. } Happy return be to your royal Grace!

DUKE. Many and hearty thankings to you both.
   We have made inquiry of you; and we hear
   Such goodness of your justice, that our soul
   Cannot but yield you forth to public thanks,
   Forerunning more requital.

ANG.   You make my bonds still greater.

DUKE. O, your desert speaks loud; and I should wrong it,
   To lock it in the wards of covert bosom,
   When it deserves, with characters of brass,
   A forted residence 'gainst the tooth of time
   And razure of oblivion. Give me your hand,
   And let the subject see, to make them know
   That outward courtesies would fain proclaim
   Favours that keep within.[1] Come, Escalus;
   You must walk by us on our other hand:
   And good supporters are you.

FRIAR PETER *and* ISABELLA *come forward*

FRI. P. Now is your time: speak loud, and kneel before him.

[1]*Favours . . . within*] Marks of recognition that are in my heart.

ISAB.   Justice, O royal Duke! Vail your regard[2]
    Upon a wrong'd, I would fain have said, a maid!
    O worthy prince, dishonour not your eye
    By throwing it on any other object
    Till you have heard me in my true complaint,
    And given me justice, justice, justice, justice!
DUKE.   Relate your wrongs; in what? by whom? be brief.
    Here is Lord Angelo shall give you justice:
    Reveal yourself to him.
ISAB.   O worthy Duke,
    You bid me seek redemption of the devil:
    Hear me yourself; for that which I must speak
    Must either punish me, not being believed,
    Or wring redress from you. Hear me, O hear me, here!
ANG.   My lord, her wits, I fear me, are not firm:
    She hath been a suitor to me for her brother
    Cut off by course of justice,—
ISAB.   By course of justice!
ANG.   And she will speak most bitterly and strange.
ISAB.   Most strange, but yet most truly, will I speak:
    That Angelo's forsworn; is it not strange?
    That Angelo's a murderer; is 't not strange?
    That Angelo is an adulterous thief,
    An hypocrite, a virgin-violator;
    Is it not strange and strange?
DUKE.   Nay, it is ten times strange.
ISAB.   It is not truer he is Angelo
    Than this is all as true as it is strange:
    Nay, it is ten times true; for truth is truth
    To the end of reckoning.
DUKE.   Away with her!—Poor soul,
    She speaks this in the infirmity of sense.
ISAB.   O prince, I conjure thee, as thou believest
    There is another comfort than this world,
    That thou neglect me not, with that opinion
    That I am touch'd with madness! Make not impossible
    That which but seems unlike: 't is not impossible
    But one, the wicked'st caitiff on the ground,
    May seem as shy, as grave, as just, as absolute[3]
    As Angelo; even so may Angelo,

[2]*Vail your regard*] Lower your eyes. Cf. *Venus and Adonis*, 956, "She *vail'd* her eyelids."
[3]*shy . . . absolute*] modestly reserved . . . perfect.

In all his dressings, characts,[4] titles, forms,
Be an arch-villain; believe it, royal prince:
If he be less, he's nothing; but he's more,
Had I more name for badness.

DUKE.   By mine honesty,
If she be mad,—as I believe no other,—
Her madness hath the oddest frame of sense,
Such a dependency of thing on thing,
As e'er I heard in madness.

ISAB.   O gracious Duke,
Harp not on that; nor do not banish reason
For inequality;[5] but let your reason serve
To make the truth appear where it seems hid,
And hide the false seems true.[6]

DUKE.   Many that are not mad
Have, sure, more lack of reason. What would you say?

ISAB.   I am the sister of one Claudio,
Condemn'd upon the act of fornication
To lose his head; condemn'd by Angelo:
I, in probation of a sisterhood,
Was sent to by my brother; one Lucio
As then the messenger,—

LUCIO.   That's I, an 't like your Grace:
I came to her from Claudio, and desired her
To try her gracious fortune with Lord Angelo
For her poor brother's pardon.

ISAB.   That's he indeed.

DUKE.   You were not bid to speak.

LUCIO.   No, my good lord;
Nor wish'd to hold my peace.

DUKE.   I wish you now, then;
Pray you, take note of it: and when you have
A business for yourself, pray heaven you then
Be perfect.

LUCIO.   I warrant your honour.

DUKE.   The warrant's for yourself; take heed to 't.

ISAB.   This gentleman told somewhat of my tale,—

LUCIO.   Right.

---

[4]*dressings, characts*] habiliments, badges of office. "Characts" is not an uncommon abbreviation of "characters."
[5]*For inequality*] Because my speech is unequal or inconsistent.
[6]*hide the false seems true*] seclude the falsehood which now seems truth.

DUKE.   It may be right; but you are i' the wrong
    To speak before your time. Proceed.
ISAB.   I went
    To this pernicious caitiff Deputy,—
DUKE.   That's somewhat madly spoken.
ISAB.   Pardon it;
    The phrase is to the matter.
DUKE.   Mended again. The matter;—proceed.
ISAB.   In brief,—to set the needless process by,
    How I persuaded, how I pray'd, and kneel'd,
    How he refell'd[7] me, and how I replied,—
    For this was of much length,—the vile conclusion
    I now begin with grief and shame to utter:
    He would not, but by gift of my chaste body
    To his concupiscible intemperate lust,
    Release my brother; and, after much debatement,
    My sisterly remorse confutes[8] mine honour,
    And I did yield to him: but the next morn betimes,
    His purpose surfeiting, he sends a warrant
    For my poor brother's head.
DUKE.   This is most likely!
ISAB.   O, that it were as like as it is true!
DUKE.   By heaven, fond wretch, thou know'st not what thou speak'st,
    Or else thou art suborn'd against his honour
    In hateful practice. First, his integrity
    Stands without blemish. Next, it imports no reason
    That with such vehemency he should pursue
    Faults proper to himself:[9] if he had so offended,
    He would have weigh'd[10] thy brother by himself,
    And not have cut him off. Some one hath set you on:
    Confess the truth, and say by whose advice
    Thou camest here to complain.
ISAB.   And is this all?
    Then, O you blessed ministers above,
    Keep me in patience, and with ripen'd time
    Unfold the evil which is here wrapt up

---

[7]*refell'd*] refuted.
[8]*My sisterly . . . confutes*] My sisterly pity overthrows.
[9]*it imports . . . to himself*] there is no cause in reason why he should attack with such
  vehemence faults inherent in himself.
[10]*weigh'd*] judged.

In countenance![11] — Heaven shield your Grace from woe,
As I, thus wrong'd, hence unbelieved go!
DUKE.   I know you 'ld fain be gone. — An officer!
To prison with her! — Shall we thus permit
A blasting and a scandalous breath to fall
On him so near us? This needs must be a practice.
Who knew of your intent and coming hither?
ISAB.   One that I would were here, Friar Lodowick.
DUKE.   A ghostly father, belike. Who knows that Lodowick?
LUCIO.   My lord, I know him; 't is a meddling friar;
I do not like the man: had he been lay, my lord,
For certain words he spake against your Grace
In your retirement, I had swinged him soundly.
DUKE.   Words against me! this 's a good friar, belike!
And to set on this wretched woman here
Against our substitute! Let this friar be found.
LUCIO.   But yesternight, my lord, she and that friar,
I saw them at the prison: a saucy friar,
A very scurvy fellow.
FRI. P.   Blessed be your royal Grace!
I have stood by, my lord, and I have heard
Your royal ear abused. First, hath this woman
Most wrongfully accused your substitute,
Who is as free from touch or soil with her
As she from one ungot.
DUKE.   We did believe no less.
Know you that Friar Lodowick that she speaks of?
FRI. P.   I know him for a man divine and holy;
Not scurvy, nor a temporary meddler,[12]
As he's reported by this gentleman;
And, on my trust, a man that never yet
Did, as he vouches, misreport your Grace.
LUCIO.   My lord, most villainously; believe it.
FRI. P.   Well, he in time may come to clear himself;
But at this instant he is sick, my lord,
Of a strange fever. Upon his mere request, —
Being come to knowledge that there was complaint
Intended 'gainst Lord Angelo, — came I hither,
To speak, as from his mouth, what he doth know
Is true and false; and what he with his oath

---

[11]*wrapt up . . . In countenance*] concealed owing to the countenance or partiality extended to the offender.
[12]*a temporary meddler*] one who meddles in temporal or secular affairs.

And all probation will make up full clear,
Whensoever he's convented.[13] First, for this woman,
To justify this worthy nobleman,
So vulgarly and personally accused,
Her shall you hear disproved to her eyes,
Till she herself confess it.

DUKE.   Good friar, let's hear it.

     [ISABELLA *is carried off guarded; and* MARIANA *comes forward.*
Do you not smile at this, Lord Angelo?—
O heaven, the vanity of wretched fools!—
Give us some seats. Come, cousin Angelo;
In this I'll be impartial; be you judge
Of your own cause. Is this the witness, friar?
First, let her show her face, and after speak.

MARI.   Pardon, my lord; I will not show my face
Until my husband bid me.

DUKE.   What, are you married?

MARI.   No, my lord.

DUKE.   Are you a maid?

MARI.   No, my lord.

DUKE.   A widow, then?

MARI.   Neither, my lord.

DUKE.   Why, you are nothing, then:—neither maid, widow, nor wife?

LUCIO.   My lord, she may be a punk; for many of them are neither
maid, widow, nor wife.

DUKE.   Silence that fellow: I would he had some cause
To prattle for himself.

LUCIO.   Well, my lord.

MARI.   My lord, I do confess I ne'er was married;
And I confess, besides, I am no maid:
I have known my husband; yet my husband
Knows not that ever he knew me.

LUCIO.   He was drunk, then, my lord: it can be no better.

DUKE.   For the benefit of silence, would thou wert so too!

LUCIO.   Well, my lord.

DUKE.   This is no witness for Lord Angelo.

MARI.   Now I come to 't, my lord:
She that accuses him of fornication,
In self-same manner doth accuse my husband;
And charges him, my lord, with such a time

---

[13]*convented*] summoned. Cf. *Cor.*, II, ii, 58–59: "We are *convented* Upon a pleasant treaty."

When I'll depose I had him in mine arms
With all the effect of love.
ANG. Charges she more than me?
MARI.   Not that I know.
DUKE. No? you say your husband.
MARI. Why, just, my lord, and that is Angelo,
Who thinks he knows that he ne'er knew my body,
But knows he thinks that he knows Isabel's.
ANG. This is a strange abuse. Let's see thy face.
MARI. My husband bids me; now I will unmask.   [*Unveiling.*
This is that face, thou cruel Angelo,
Which once thou sworest was worth the looking on;
This is the hand which, with a vow'd contract,
Was fast belock'd in thine; this is the body
That took away the match from Isabel,
And did supply thee at thy garden-house
In her imagined person.
DUKE.   Know you this woman?
LUCIO. Carnally, she says.
DUKE.   Sirrah, no more!
LUCIO. Enough, my lord.
ANG. My lord, I must confess I know this woman:
And five years since there was some speech of marriage
Betwixt myself and her; which was broke off,
Partly for that her promised proportions
Came short of composition;[14] but in chief,
For that her reputation was disvalued
In levity:[15] since which time of five years
I never spake with her, saw her, nor heard from her,
Upon my faith and honour.
MARI.   Noble prince,
As there comes light from heaven and words from breath,
As there is sense in truth and truth in virtue,
I am affianced this man's wife as strongly
As words could make up vows: and, my good lord,
But Tuesday night last gone in 's garden-house
He knew me as a wife. As this is true,
Let me in safety raise me from my knees;
Or else for ever be confixed here,
A marble monument!

[14]*her promised . . . composition*] her promised portion or dowry fell short of the agreement. Cf. *Two Gent.*, II, iii, 3: "I have received my *proportion.*"
[15]*her reputation . . . levity*] her good name was depreciated owing to her loose behavior.

ANG.   I did but smile till now:
    Now, good my lord, give me the scope of justice;
    My patience here is touch'd. I do perceive
    These poor informal[16] women are no more
    But instruments of some more mightier member
    That sets them on: let me have way, my lord,
    To find this practice out.
DUKE.   Ay, with my heart;
    And punish them to your height of pleasure.
    Thou foolish friar; and thou pernicious woman,
    Compact with her that's gone, think'st thou thy oaths,
    Though they would swear down each particular saint,
    Were testimonies against his worth and credit,
    That's seal'd in approbation?[17] You, Lord Escalus,
    Sit with my cousin; lend him your kind pains
    To find out this abuse, whence 't is derived.
    There is another friar that set them on;
    Let him be sent for.
FRI. P.   Would he were here, my lord! for he, indeed,
    Hath set the women on to this complaint:
    Your provost knows the place where he abides,
    And he may fetch him.
DUKE.   Go, do it instantly.   [*Exit* PROVOST.
    And you, my noble and well-warranted cousin,
    Whom it concerns to hear this matter forth,[18]
    Do with your injuries as seems you best,
    In any chastisement: I for a while will leave you;
    But stir not you till you have well determined
    Upon these slanderers.
ESCAL.   My lord, we'll do it throughly. [*Exit* DUKE.] Signior Lucio,
    did not you say you knew that Friar Lodowick to be a dishonest
    person?
LUCIO.   "Cucullus non facit monachum":[19] honest in nothing but in
    his clothes; and one that hath spoke most villainous speeches of
    the Duke.

---

[16]*informal*] crazy, irrational; an uncommon usage, though "formal" is frequently used
  by Shakespeare in the sense of "rational." Cf. *Ant. and Cleop.*, II, v, 41: "Thou
  shouldst come like a Fury . . . Not like a *formal* man."

[17]*seal'd in approbation*] ratified or certified by proof. The seal is the final mark of legal
  validity.

[18]*hear . . . forth*] hear out, hear to the end.

[19]"*Cucullus . . . monachum*"] This familiar Latin proverb already has been quoted
  by Shakespeare in *Tw. Night*, I, v, 50. It is translated in *Hen. VIII*, III, i, 23: "all
  hoods make not monks."

ESCAL. We shall entreat you to abide here till he come, and enforce
  them against him: we shall find this friar a notable fellow.

LUCIO. As any in Vienna, on my word.

ESCAL. Call that same Isabel here once again: I would speak with
  her. [*Exit an* Attendant.] Pray you, my lord, give me leave to question; you shall see how I'll handle her.

LUCIO. Not better than he, by her own report.

ESCAL. Say you?

LUCIO. Marry, sir, I think, if you handled her privately, she would
  sooner confess: perchance, publicly, she'll be ashamed.

ESCAL. I will go darkly to work with her.

LUCIO. That's the way; for women are light at midnight.[20]

Re-enter Officers *with* ISABELLA; *and* PROVOST *with the* DUKE *in his
friar's habit*

ESCAL. Come on, mistress: here's a gentlewoman denies all that you
  have said.

LUCIO. My lord, here comes the rascal I spoke of; here with the
  provost.

ESCAL. In very good time: speak not you to him till we call upon you.

LUCIO. Mum.

ESCAL. Come, sir: did you set these women on to slander Lord
  Angelo? they have confessed you did.

DUKE. 'T is false.

ESCAL. How! know you where you are?

DUKE. Respect to your great place! and let the devil
  Be sometime honour'd for his burning throne!
  Where is the Duke? 't is he should hear me speak.

ESCAL. The Duke's in us; and we will hear you speak:
  Look you speak justly.

DUKE. Boldly, at least. But, O, poor souls,
  Come you to seek the lamb here of the fox?
  Good night to your redress! Is the Duke gone?
  Then is your cause gone too. The Duke's unjust,
  Thus to retort your manifest appeal,[21]
  And put your trial in the villain's mouth
  Which here you come to accuse.

LUCIO. This is the rascal; this is he I spoke of.

ESCAL. Why, thou unreverend and unhallow'd friar,

---

[20]*light at midnight*] A favorite pun with Shakespeare. Cf. *Merch. of Ven.*, V, i, 129: "Let
me give *light*, but let me not be *light*."

[21]*retort . . . appeal*] refer back to Angelo your deliberate appeal to the Duke against
Angelo.

Is 't not enough thou hast suborn'd these women
To accuse this worthy man, but, in foul mouth,
And in the witness of his proper ear,
To call him villain? and then to glance from him
To the Duke himself, to tax him with injustice?
Take him hence; to the rack with him! We'll touse you
Joint by joint, but we will know his purpose.
What, "unjust"!

DUKE.   Be not so hot; the Duke
Dare no more stretch this finger of mine than he
Dare rack his own: his subject am I not,
Nor here provincial.[22] My business in this state
Made me a looker-on here in Vienna,
Where I have seen corruption boil and bubble
Till it o'er-run the stew;[23] laws for all faults,
But faults so countenanced, that the strong statutes
Stand like the forfeits in a barber's shop,[24]
As much in mock as mark.

ESCAL.   Slander to the state! Away with him to prison!

ANG.   What can you vouch against him, Signior Lucio?
Is this the man that you did tell us of?

LUCIO.   'T is he, my lord. Come hither, goodman baldpate: do you
know me?

DUKE.   I remember you, sir, by the sound of your voice: I met you at
the prison, in the absence of the Duke.

LUCIO.   O, did you so? And do you remember what you said of the
Duke?

DUKE.   Most notedly, sir.

LUCIO.   Do you so, sir? And was the Duke a flesh-monger, a fool, and
a coward, as you then reported him to be?

DUKE.   You must, sir, change persons with me, ere you make that my
report: you, indeed, spoke so of him; and much more, much
worse.

LUCIO.   O thou damnable fellow! Did not I pluck thee by the nose for
thy speeches?

DUKE.   I protest I love the Duke as I love myself.

---

[22]*his subject . . . provincial*] I am not the Duke's subject, nor amenable to the jurisdiction of the ecclesiastical authorities of the province or district.

[23]*stew*] In this culinary metaphor "stew" seems used for the "stew pan," or contents of a saucepan, with a punning allusion to "stews," *i.e.*, brothels.

[24]*the forfeits in a barber's shop*] lists of petty fines or forfeits, often of farcical character, which hung on the walls of a barber's shop. They were playfully intended to keep order among the customers.

ANG.   Hark, how the villain would close[25] now, after his treasonable abuses!

ESCAL.   Such a fellow is not to be talked withal. Away with him to prison! Where is the provost? Away with him to prison! lay bolts enough upon him: let him speak no more. Away with those giglets[26] too, and with the other confederate companion!

DUKE.   [*To the* PROVOST] Stay, sir; stay awhile.

ANG.   What, resists he? Help him, Lucio.

LUCIO.   Come, sir; come, sir; come, sir; foh, sir! Why, you bald-pated, lying rascal, you must be hooded, must you? Show your knave's visage, with a pox to you! show your sheep-biting face, and be hanged an hour![27] Will 't not off?

> [*Pulls off the friar's hood, and discovers the* DUKE.

DUKE.   Thou art the first knave that e'er madest a Duke.
First, provost, let me bail these gentle three.
[*To* LUCIO] Sneak not away, sir; for the friar and you
Must have a word anon. Lay hold on him.

LUCIO.   This may prove worse than hanging.

DUKE.   [*To* ESCALUS] What you have spoke I pardon: sit you down:
We'll borrow place of him. [*To* ANGELO] Sir, by your leave.
Hast thou or word, or wit, or impudence,
That yet can do thee office?[28] If thou hast,
Rely upon it till my tale be heard,
And hold no longer out.

ANG.   O my dread lord,
I should be guiltier than my guiltiness,
To think I can be undiscernible, ·
When I perceive your Grace, like power divine,
Hath look'd upon my passes.[29] Then, good prince,
No longer session hold upon my shame,
But let my trial be mine own confession:
Immediate sentence then, and sequent death,
Is all the grace I beg.

DUKE.   Come hither, Mariana.
Say, wast thou e'er contracted to this woman?

ANG.   I was, my lord.

---

[25]*close*] Cf. *Troil. and Cress.*, III, ii, 47: "an 't were dark, you 'ld *close* [*i.e.*, come to terms] sooner."

[26]*giglets*] Cf. 1 *Hen. VI*, IV, vii, 41: "a *giglot* [*i.e.*, wanton] wench."

[27]*sheep-biting face . . . hour!*] A "sheep-biter" is a sneaking cur that worries sheep. "An hour" seems here an emphatic synonym for "a while."

[28]*can do thee office?*] can do thee service?

[29]*passes*] The word here is almost equivalent to "trespass." But there is an allusion to the passes (*i.e.*, tricks) of jugglery.

DUKE.   Go take her hence, and marry her instantly.
Do you the office, friar; which consummate,
Return him here again. Go with him, provost.
          [*Exeunt* ANGELO, MARIANA, FRIAR PETER, *and* PROVOST.
ESCAL.   My lord, I am more amazed at his dishonour
Than at the strangeness of it.
DUKE.   Come hither, Isabel.
Your friar is now your prince: as I was then
Advertising[30] and holy to your business,
Not changing heart with habit, I am still
Attorney'd at your service.
ISAB.   O, give me pardon,
That I, your vassal, have employ'd and pain'd[31]
Your unknown sovereignty!
DUKE.   You are pardon'd, Isabel:
And now, dear maid, be you as free to us.
Your brother's death, I know, sits at your heart;
And you may marvel why I obscured myself,
Labouring to save his life, and would not rather
Make rash remonstrance[32] of my hidden power
Than let him so be lost. O most kind maid,
It was the swift celerity of his death,
Which I did think with slower foot came on,
That brain'd my purpose.[33] But, peace be with him!
That life is better life, past fearing death,
Than that which lives to fear: make it your comfort,
So happy is your brother.
ISAB.   I do, my lord.

Re-enter ANGELO, MARIANA, FRIAR PETER, *and* PROVOST

DUKE.   For this new-married man, approaching here,
Whose salt imagination[34] yet hath wrong'd
Your well-defended honour, you must pardon
For Mariana's sake: but as he adjudged your brother,—
Being criminal, in double violation
Of sacred chastity, and of promise-breach

[30]*Advertising . . . business*] Counselling, and faithful to your affairs.

[31]*employ'd and pain'd*] given trouble to, given cause for labor. "Painful" is frequently found in the sense of "laborious."

[32]*rash remonstrance*] hasty demonstration, manifestation, display.

[33]*brain'd my purpose*] knocked my desire on the head. Cf. *Tempest*, III, ii, 84: "thou mayst *brain* him."

[34]*salt imagination*] Cf. *Othello*, II, i, 237: "His *salt* [*i.e.*, lustful] and most hidden loose affection."

Thereon dependent, for your brother's life,[35]—
The very mercy of the law cries out
Most audible, even from his proper tongue,
"An Angelo for Claudio, death for death!"
Haste still pays haste, and leisure answers leisure;
Like doth quit like, and MEASURE still FOR MEASURE.[36]
Then, Angelo, thy fault's thus manifested;
Which, though thou wouldst deny, denies thee vantage.[37]
We do condemn thee to the very block
Where Claudio stoop'd to death, and with like haste.
Away with him!

MARI. O my most gracious lord,
 I hope you will not mock me with a husband.

DUKE. It is your husband mock'd you with a husband.
 Consenting to the safeguard of your honour,
 I thought your marriage fit; else imputation,
 For that he knew you, might reproach your life,
 And choke your good to come: for his possessions,
 Although by confiscation[38] they are ours,
 We do instate and widow[39] you withal,
 To buy you a better husband.

MARI. O my dear lord,
 I crave no other, nor no better man.

DUKE. Never crave him; we are definitive.

MARI. Gentle my liege,—   [*Kneeling.*

DUKE. You do but lose your labour.
 Away with him to death! [*To* LUCIO] Now, sir, to you.

MARI. O my good lord! Sweet Isabel, take my part;
 Lend me your knees, and all my life to come
 I'll lend you all my life to do you service.

DUKE. Against all sense you do importune her:
 Should she kneel down in mercy of this fact,[40]

---

[35]*Being criminal . . . life*] The language is irregular. The meaning is that Angelo was guilty of two crimes: first, of violating sacred chastity, and then of breaking the promise given to preserve the brother's life.

[36]*Measure . . . for Measure*] A proverbial expression equivalent to "tit for tat." Cf. 3 *Hen. VI*, II, vi, 55: "*Measure for measure* must be answered."

[37]*Which . . . vantage*] The denial of which is no advantage to thee. Cf. *Wint. Tale*, III, ii, 84: "Which to deny concerns more than avails."

[38]*confiscation*] Thus the Second and later Folios. The First Folio reads *confutation*, which has been explained to mean "conviction," "confutare" being found in the sense of "to convict" in post-classical authors.

[39]*instate and widow*] confer as the dower or jointure of a widow.

[40]*in mercy of this fact*] by way of pardoning this deed or crime.

Her brother's ghost his paved bed would break,
And take her hence in horror.

MARI.   Isabel,
     Sweet Isabel, do yet but kneel by me;
     Hold up your hands, say nothing, I'll speak all.
     They say, best men are moulded out of faults;
     And, for the most, become much more the better
     For being a little bad: so may my husband.
     O Isabel, will you not lend a knee?

DUKE.   He dies for Claudio's death.

ISAB.   Most bounteous sir,   [*Kneeling*.
     Look, if it please you, on this man condemn'd,
     As if my brother lived: I partly think
     A due sincerity govern'd his deeds,
     Till he did look on me: since it is so,
     Let him not die. My brother had but justice,   *z*
     In that he did the thing for which he died:
     For Angelo,
     His act did not o'ertake his bad intent;[41]
     And must be buried but as an intent
     That perish'd by the way: thoughts are no subjects;
     Intents, but merely thoughts.

MARI.   Merely, my lord.

DUKE.   Your suit's unprofitable; stand up, I say.
     I have bethought me of another fault.
     Provost, how came it Claudio was beheaded
     At an unusual hour?

PROV.   It was commanded so.

DUKE.   Had you a special warrant for the deed?

PROV.   No, my good lord; it was by private message.

DUKE.   For which I do discharge you of your office:
     Give up your keys.

PROV.   Pardon me, noble lord:
     I thought it was a fault, but knew it not;
     Yet did repent me, after more advice:[42]
     For testimony whereof, one in the prison,
     That should by private order else have died,
     I have reserved alive.

DUKE.   What's he?

PROV.   His name is Barnardine.

---

[41]*His act . . . intent*] Cf. *Macb.*, IV, i, 145–146. "The flighty *purpose* never is *o'ertook*
   Unless the *deed* go with it."
[42]*after more advice*] on further consideration.

DUKE.   I would thou hadst done so by Claudio.
    Go fetch him hither; let me look upon him.   [*Exit* PROVOST.
ESCAL.   I am sorry, one so learned and so wise
    As you, Lord Angelo, have still appear'd,
    Should slip so grossly, both in the heat of blood,
    And lack of temper'd judgement afterward.
ANG.   I am sorry that such sorrow I procure:
    And so deep sticks it in my penitent heart,
    That I crave death more willingly than mercy;
    'T is my deserving, and I do entreat it.

Re-enter PROVOST, *with* BARNARDINE, CLAUDIO *muffled, and* JULIET

DUKE.   Which is that Barnardine?
PROV.   This, my lord.
DUKE.   There was a friar told me of this man.
    Sirrah, thou art said to have a stubborn soul,
    That apprehends no further than this world,
    And squarest thy life according. Thou'rt condemn'd:
    But, for those earthly faults, I quit them all;[43]
    And pray thee take this mercy to provide
    For better times to come. Friar, advise him;
    I leave him to your hand. What muffled fellow's that?
PROV.   This is another prisoner that I saved,
    Who should have died when Claudio lost his head;
    As like almost to Claudio as himself.   [*Unmuffles* CLAUDIO.
DUKE.   [*To* ISABELLA] If he be like your brother, for his sake
    Is he pardon'd; and, for your lovely sake,
    Give me your hand, and say you will be mine,
    He is my brother too:[44] but fitter time for that.
    By this Lord Angelo perceives he's safe;
    Methinks I see a quickening in his eye.
    Well, Angelo, your evil quits you well:[45]
    Look that you love your wife; her worth worth yours.
    I find an apt remission[46] in myself;
    And yet here's one in place I cannot pardon.
    [*To* LUCIO] You, sirrah, that knew me for a fool, a coward,
    One all of luxury, an ass, a madman;

[43]*But . . . all*] But for those faults punishable on earth, cognizable by temporal power, I forgive them all.
[44]*Give me . . . brother too*] These lines are somewhat elliptical. The Duke seems to mean that provided Isabella give him her hand, Claudio will then be his brother too. Isabella expresses no emotion verbally on finding Claudio alive. Much is left to be supplied by the gestures of the actors.
[45]*your evil quits you well*] your ill-doing lets you off easily.
[46]*an apt remission*] an inclination to pardon.

Wherein have I so deserved of you,
That you extol me thus?

LUCIO. 'Faith, my lord, I spoke it but according to the trick.[47] If you
will hang me for it, you may; but I had rather it would please you
I might be whipt.

DUKE. Whipt first, sir, and hang'd after.
Proclaim it, provost, round about the city,
If any woman wrong'd by this lewd fellow,—
As I have heard him swear himself there's one
Whom he begot with child, let her appear,
And he shall marry her: the nuptial finish'd,
Let him be whipt and hang'd.

LUCIO. I beseech your highness, do not marry me to a whore. Your
highness said even now, I made you a Duke: good my lord, do not
recompense me in making me a cuckold.

DUKE. Upon mine honour, thou shalt marry her.
Thy slanders I forgive; and therewithal
Remit thy other forfeits.[48]—Take him to prison;
And see our pleasure herein executed.

LUCIO. Marrying a punk, my lord, is pressing to death,[49] whipping,
and hanging.

DUKE. Slandering a prince deserves it.

                                       [*Exeunt* Officers *with* LUCIO.

She, Claudio, that you wrong'd, look you restore.
Joy to you, Mariana! Love her, Angelo:
I have confess'd her, and I know her virtue.
Thanks, good friend Escalus, for thy much goodness:
There's more behind that is more gratulate.[50]
Thanks, provost, for thy care and secrecy:
We shall employ thee in a worthier place.
Forgive him, Angelo, that brought you home
The head of Ragozine for Claudio's:
The offence pardons itself. Dear Isabel,
I have a motion much imports your good;
Whereto if you'll a willing ear incline,
What's mine is yours, and what is yours is mine.
So, bring us to our palace; where we'll show
What's yet behind, that's meet you all should know.

                                                  [*Exeunt.*

---

[47]*according to the trick*] according to sportive custom, thoughtlessly.

[48]*forfeits*] punishments, penalties.

[49]*pressing to death*] This was the cruel punishment dealt out, according to English law, to persons accused of felony who refused to plead.

[50]*more gratulate*] more to be rejoiced at, more worthy of congratulation.

DOVER · THRIFT · EDITIONS

NONFICTION

A MODEST PROPOSAL AND OTHER SATIRICAL WORKS, Jonathan Swift. 64pp. 28759-9 $1.00
UTOPIA, Sir Thomas More. 96pp. 29583-4 $1.50
THE AUTOBIOGRAPHY OF BENJAMIN FRANKLIN, Benjamin Franklin. 144pp. 29073-5 $1.50
COMMON SENSE, Thomas Paine. 64pp. 29602-4 $1.00
THE STORY OF MY LIFE, Helen Keller. 80pp. 29249-5 $1.00
GREAT SPEECHES, Abraham Lincoln. 112pp. 26872-1 $1.00
THE PRINCE, Niccolò Machiavelli. 80pp. 27274-5 $1.00
PRAGMATISM, William James. 128pp. 28270-8 $1.50
TOTEM AND TABOO, Sigmund Freud. 176pp. (Available in U.S. only) 40434-X $2.00
POETICS, Aristotle. 64pp. 29577-X $1.00
NICOMACHEAN ETHICS, Aristotle. 256pp. 40096-4 $2.00
MEDITATIONS, Marcus Aurelius. 128pp. 29823-X $1.50
SYMPOSIUM AND PHAEDRUS, Plato. 96pp. 27798-4 $1.50
THE TRIAL AND DEATH OF SOCRATES: Four Dialogues, Plato. 128pp. 27066-1 $1.00
THE BIRTH OF TRAGEDY, Friedrich Nietzsche. 96pp. 28515-4 $1.50
BEYOND GOOD AND EVIL: Prelude to a Philosophy of the Future, Friedrich Nietzsche. 176pp. 29868-X $1.50
CONFESSIONS OF AN ENGLISH OPIUM EATER, Thomas De Quincey. 80pp. 28742-4 $1.00
CIVIL DISOBEDIENCE AND OTHER ESSAYS, Henry David Thoreau. 96pp. 27563-9 $1.00
SELECTIONS FROM THE JOURNALS (Edited by Walter Harding), Herny David Thoreau. 96pp. 28760-2 $1.00
WALDEN; OR, LIFE IN THE WOODS, Henry David Thoreau. 224pp. 28495-6 $2.00
THE LAND OF LITTLE RAIN, Mary Austin. 96pp. 29037-9 $1.50
THE THEORY OF THE LEISURE CLASS, Thorstein Veblen. 256pp. 28062-4 $2.00

PLAYS

PROMETHEUS BOUND, Aeschylus. 64pp. 28762-9 $1.00
THE ORESTEIA TRILOGY: Agamemnon, The Libation-Bearers and The Furies, Aeschylus. 160pp. 29242-8 $1.50
LYSISTRATA, Aristophanes. 64pp. 28225-2 $1.00
WHAT EVERY WOMAN KNOWS, James Barrie. 80pp. (Available in U.S. only) 29578-8 $1.50
THE CHERRY ORCHARD, Anton Chekhov. 64pp. 26682-6 $1.00
THE THREE SISTERS, Anton Chekhov. 64pp. 27544-2 $1.00
UNCLE VANYA, Anton Chekhov. 64pp. 40159-6 $1.50
THE INSPECTOR GENERAL, Nikolai Gogol. 80pp. 28500-6 $1.50
THE WAY OF THE WORLD, William Congreve. 80pp. 27787-9 $1.50
BACCHAE, Euripides. 64pp. 29580-X $1.00
MEDEA, Euripides. 64pp. 27548-5 $1.00
THE MIKADO, William Schwenck Gilbert. 64pp. 27268-0 $1.50
FAUST, PART ONE, Johann Wolfgang von Goethe. 192pp. 28046-2 $2.00
SHE STOOPS TO CONQUER, Oliver Goldsmith. 80pp. 26867-5 $1.50
A DOLL'S HOUSE, Henrik Ibsen. 80pp. 27062-9 $1.00
HEDDA GABLER, Henrik Ibsen. 80pp. 26469-6 $1.50
GHOSTS, Henrik Ibsen. 64pp. 29852-3 $1.50
VOLPONE, Ben Jonson. 112pp. 28049-7 $1.50
DR. FAUSTUS, Christopher Marlowe. 64pp. 28208-2 $1.00
THE MISANTHROPE, Molière. 64pp. 27065-3 $1.00

DOVER · THRIFT · EDITIONS

PLAYS

THE EMPEROR JONES, Eugene O'Neill. 64pp. 29268-1 $1.50

BEYOND THE HORIZON, Eugene O'Neill. 96pp. 29085-9 $1.50

ANNA CHRISTIE, Eugene O'Neill. 80pp. 29985-6 $1.50

THE LONG VOYAGE HOME AND OTHER PLAYS, Eugene O'Neill. 80pp. 28755-6 $1.00

RIGHT YOU ARE, IF YOU THINK YOU ARE, Luigi Pirandello. 64pp. (Available in U.S. only) 29576-1 $1.50

SIX CHARACTERS IN SEARCH OF AN AUTHOR, Luigi Pirandello. 64pp. (Available in U.S. only) 29992-9 $1.50

HANDS AROUND, Arthur Schnitzler. 64pp. 28724-6 $1.00

ANTONY AND CLEOPATRA, William Shakespeare. 128pp. 40062-X $1.50

HAMLET, William Shakespeare. 128pp. 27278-8 $1.00

HENRY IV, William Shakespeare. 96pp. 29584-2 $1.00

RICHARD III, William Shakespeare. 112pp. 28747-5 $1.00

OTHELLO, William Shakespeare. 112pp. 29097-2 $1.00

JULIUS CAESAR, William Shakespeare. 80pp. 26876-4 $1.00

KING LEAR, William Shakespeare. 112pp. 28058-6 $1.00

MACBETH, William Shakespeare. 96pp. 27802-6 $1.00

THE MERCHANT OF VENICE, William Shakespeare. 96pp. 28492-1 $1.00

A MIDSUMMER NIGHT'S DREAM, William Shakespeare. 80pp. 27067-X $1.00

MUCH ADO ABOUT NOTHING, William Shakespeare. 80pp. 28272-4 $1.00

AS YOU LIKE IT, William Shakespeare. 80pp. 40432-3 $1.50

THE TAMING OF THE SHREW, William Shakespeare. 96pp. 29765-9 $1.00

TWELFTH NIGHT; OR, WHAT YOU WILL, William Shakespeare. 80pp. 29290-8 $1.00

ROMEO AND JULIET, William Shakespeare. 96pp. 27557-4 $1.00

ARMS AND THE MAN, George Bernard Shaw. 80pp. (Available in U.S. only) 26476-9 $1.50

PYGMALION, George Bernard Shaw. 96pp. (Available in U.S. only) 28222-8 $1.00

HEARTBREAK HOUSE, George Bernard Shaw. 128pp. (Available in U.S. only) 29291-6 $1.50

THE SCHOOL FOR SCANDAL, Richard Brinsley Sheridan. 96pp. 26687-7 $1.50

ANTIGONE, Sophocles. 64pp. 27804-2 $1.00

OEDIPUS REX, Sophocles. 64pp. 26877-2 $1.00

ELECTRA, Sophocles. 64pp. 28482-4 $1.00

MISS JULIE, August Strindberg. 64pp. 27281-8 $1.50

THE PLAYBOY OF THE WESTERN WORLD AND RIDERS TO THE SEA, J. M. Synge. 80pp. 27562-0 $1.50

THE IMPORTANCE OF BEING EARNEST, Oscar Wilde. 64pp. 26478-5 $1.00

LADY WINDERMERE'S FAN, Oscar Wilde. 64pp. 40078-6 $1.00

BOXED SETS

FIVE GREAT POETS: Poems by Shakespeare, Keats, Poe, Dickinson and Whitman, Dover. 416pp. 26942-6 $5.00

NINE GREAT ENGLISH POETS: Poems by Shakespeare, Keats, Blake, Coleridge, Wordsworth, Mrs. Browning, FitzGerald, Tennyson and Kipling, Dover. 704pp. 27633-3 $9.00

FIVE GREAT ENGLISH ROMANTIC POETS, Dover. 496pp. 27893-X $5.00

SEVEN GREAT ENGLISH VICTORIAN POETS: Seven Volumes, Dover. 592pp. 40204-5 $7.50

SIX GREAT AMERICAN POETS: Poems by Poe, Dickinson, Whitman, Longfellow, Frost and Millay, Dover. 512pp. (Available in U.S. only) 27425-X $6.00